# Grifty Shades of Fey

Cautionary Tales Uncovering the Dark Side of the Fair Folk

A Grifty Shades of Fey Anthology:
Volume One

Edited by
Michael C. Cluff

Grifty Shades of Fey:
Cautionary Tales Uncovering the Dark Side of the Fair Folk



Paperback Edition
ISBN: 978-1-947655-53-9

Published by Fiction Vortex, Inc. (FV Press)
Nampa, ID 83651
http://www.fictionvortex.com

Cover art by Niels Christensen
*Published in the United States of America*

For those who still seek the Fair Folk, tricks and all...

## Table of Contents

# Introduction

I am writing this bit of an introduction in an undisclosed location. Ever since I actively promoted *Grifty Shades of Fey*, life has been… interesting. I can't, with absolute certainty, lay the blame for the events of the last eight months at the feet of the Fair Folk, but I am taking necessary precautions.

Unexpected spikes in fertility—leading to the ever-expanding growth in my wife's abdomen; virulent wanderlust—an unexpected relocation of Cluff-central, with subsequent unforeseen remodels and repairs. Those events, while not necessarily malevolent in nature, have led to delays in the production of this project.

It is common knowledge amongst believers (look to the Egyptians and Sarah A. Hoyt's story in this collection) that cats simultaneously exist in both the mortal and ethereal realms—and that they act as guardians for the veil-blinded, we humans. Not of a coincidence, I do believe that the Fey did orchestrate the abduction of our two cats, Dodge (an old crusty bachelor of an orange tabby) and Fritzwilliam Darcy (a younger snob of a gray and black tabby). My son and I were able to rescue Fritz. However, during an unseasonal cold snap of a night, Dodge disappeared and was lost to us forever. His services are not forgotten or unappreciated.

Fritz has valiantly stepped-up in his duties in the absence of his fallen senior officer. Multiple instances of 'feather explosions' in our basement (with the absence of any blood or bodies) lead us to believe that Fritz has taken out a significant number of dark fey. We hope to provide him with a new recruit soon.

The stories included in this anthology are categorized as fiction. They have to be, for my protection, and for the protection of the authors who wrote them. It is my guarantee that deeper lessons reside within each narrative. I encourage you to read them multiple times and uncover little gems and treasures as you do. You'll find traditional narratives, stories akin to LitRPG and Yelp reviews, epistolary, and even a feline pulp memoir. All written for the greater good of humanity in a time where belief is so tenuous and swayable.

You, as the reader, have the choice to take in these stories at an entertainment level, or as a source of aforementioned deeper lessons and wisdom. Depending on your investment as you read the subsequent stories, I offer this warning: Becoming 'woke' to the schemes, plots, and dark desires of the Fey can have negative consequences, including the curse of knowledge—which really is a good thing.

Of course, I must express huge amounts of gratitude to those who helped in this project: Dawnray Ammon and Jenna Eatough and the rest of the Fyrecon crowd pitched in so much time and PR—GSOF would not have happened without them. Niels Christensen provided the art and vision behind the cover. Kasey Boles helped me focus (you really have no idea of the herculean effort that is). David Mark Brown was the one who said that my play on words needed to be an actual project. Savannah Hulen provided moral support. And my wife, Katie, is always my biggest critic and fan—she doesn't let me settle for mediocrity because she believes in me far more than I do in myself.

And then there is the multitude of Kickstarter backers: Your generosity made this a reality. I have no way of fully expressing how grateful I am to you. And I know you want to read the stories and not my blabbering.

Michael C Cluff
Fiction Vortex

# Just the Way You Are

David Farland

When Kerry decided to get his cat drunk, he had no idea how much trouble it would cause. His mom's old black Persian, Maleficent, was at death's door and constantly yowled in pain. At seventeen, a couple of years younger than Kerry, she had lost weight and arthritis swelled her joints. Oh, there were prescriptions that could offer relief, but a little whiskey in her milk took the edge off, too—and it was a lot cheaper than meds. Especially since his mom wasn't around to foot the bill.

Besides, it was fun to listen to Maleficent's confused caterwauls and watch her stagger in circles, her tail twitching like a cobra ready to strike.

The night before his anatomy final, Kerry really needed sleep, so he carried Maleficent to the utility room, poured a bit of Dead Rabbit Irish Whiskey into her red bowl along with some milk, and scratched her ears as she lapped.

When she finished, Kerry slid the backdoor open enough to air out the utility room. It was a cold-but-not-bitter Oregon night, just before Christmas, and a light snow drifted about the fields in huge flakes. He relished the cold fresh scent, and listened to the flakes shushing with thick plops. Off in the distance, a quarter mile off, "Silent Night" rose from the neighbor's house across the field. *Odd. I've never heard them play music before. Must be part of their Christmas display.*

Maleficent rubbed up against his leg, purred, then staggered into the snow to do her business.

He left the door open a couple of inches, then went to bed and lay for a while in torment. He never fell asleep easily. His stomach was cramping from nerves. He wasn't doing well in anatomy, and he'd scored lower than he wanted in organic chemistry. Oh, his scores were good solid B's, but he was hoping to get into an American med school. He needed A's, and he could feel his dreams slipping away.

He thought about going out to close the back door, call the cat in. He wished someone else was home to do it. His mom had left his dad two years ago, in part because his father was always traveling on sales business. Always traveling, week after week. So, besides Maleficent, Kerry was sole occupant of the house.

Thus he lay in bed and slid into black dreams, confused and jarring, where some creature haunted the shadowed woods behind the house. He could not see it—but he could hear it growling like distant thunder, troubling the earth.

He woke with a gasp as the house rattled, trembling so that the light fixture overhead was clanking and a picture on the wall crashed to the floor. He heard the sound again—a huge groaning noise as if a blue whale was singing. He leapt out of bed, peering around in a stupor. Red numbers flashed from his alarm clock, 3:09, and in sudden fear he ran from the room.

Earthquake, he thought. Get out! His heart raced and he rounded into the kitchen when he heard the sound again—a groan as if rocks and trees were ripping open. But he stopped short as he realized that it wasn't an earthquake. Something enormous groaned at the backdoor.

He raced into the utility room, heart hammering, and the tremendous groan emanated right at his feet, a sound so vast it rattled the foundations of the house.

He flipped on the light and beheld the source: a gray dormouse, lying with front paws draped over the cat's bowl, its nose and whiskers half submerged.

"Whoooooaaaa," the creature groaned, and the floor shuddered. "Sure and begorrah, that's a righteous drink."

I must be dreaming, Kerry stood so startled, and bewildered. Then he realized that the creature was sliding into the bowl, so he snatched the mouse up by the tail.

The mouse burped, arched its back, and stared at him drunkenly. "Ah, there's a good man," it said. The creature suddenly spasmed and its whole body trembled as it wriggled between Kerry's fingers.

In a flash, it transformed into a tiny man with glowing wings. The wings were forest green with patterns of metallic blue light, similar to the markings on an Imperial butterfly, and a large dot on each wing glowed yellow like an eye.

The little man had tan hair, the color of red wheat. Kerry held it firmly by its feet, and it smiled at him in a pleasant stupor. Its voice became soft and tinny. "Why, if it isn't Kerry O'Sullivan, in the flesh!"

"You know me?" Kerry asked.

"I know the name," the creature said. "A gift of mine. You're from a good line. Twenty generations back, your grandpappy even slew a dragon."

"Slew a dragon?"

"Och," the creature spat. "Don't tell me your people have forgotten already!"

Kerry had played just enough D&D so that he recognized a pixie when he saw it, even though it bore little resemblance to images artists put out. Instinctively he knew to grip it firmly, lest it wriggle away.

The creature grabbed Kerry's thumb and begged, "Be a good lad and set me down somewhere where I won't be underfoot."

But Kerry thought fast, recalling an old rhyme his grandmother had taught him for just such an occasion. He chanted:

"Folk be foul or folk be fair,
Don't vanish into the cool night air.
Under the Hill, you long to be,
Grant my wish, and I'll set you free!"

The little man grimaced as if Kerry had just skewered him with a fishhook. "Och, trickster—using sorcery on me!"

Its small face paled, and Kerry held it up, just watching. The little fellow had emerald green eyes and a large nose.

The cobwebs had left Kerry's mind, and he thought fast, dredging up wishes and wondering how to phrase them. I want a wish that it can't turn against me. Wisdom? No the creature would offer him tragedies. Wealth? The gold would vanish an hour after he pocketed it. Beauty?

Then it struck him, the one thing that he really wanted more than anything. It wasn't to pass his exams. He hoped to do that by himself. But there was one thing he lacked.

The pixie's face softened. "Ah, I know what you're after! I can see the wish in your heart. What's the lass's name?"

He was right. Kerry wanted love. But not with the girl who'd dumped him Saturday at dinner. He thought of a shy waif from high school, an old friend with dishwater-blonde hair and a narrow waist. She'd come over sometimes to talk or play videogames, and she'd always been so sweet.

"Delilah Kincaid?" the pixie asked and howled in glee, mocking him.

Think fast. "I know you're not supposed to grant love as a wish," Kerry said, but the pixie cut him off with a dismissive wave. "Posh! You've been watching too many—"

"But I don't want just any kind of love," Kerry demanded. "I want one that will last. I want her to love me for what I am, not like my mother—"

"Who tried to drive your father into an early grave, with all of her haranguing?"

That's it, Kerry thought. He didn't want to become his father. His mother had always set boundaries and conditions on her love, to the point where his father had called her a whore more than once.

The pixie gave a vicious smile, as if he understood far more than Kerry had explained. With a mischievous gleam in his eye he nodded. "Done!"

Kerry couldn't believe it would be so easy. "How do I know you're telling the truth?" He peered into the corner and noticed Maleficent for the first time. The cat was gazing at the pixie with huge yellow eyes, shaking as if she might perish from fright.

"Uh, that would be Delilah on the phone," the pixie said, just as the wall phone rang.

It was well after three in the morning. Kerry walked into the kitchen on wooden legs, somehow fearing that he might trip and drop the creature. He picked up the receiver in his free hand. "Hello?"

He heard Delilah's voice, somehow both timid and sultry. "Kerry?"

"Hey," he said.

She explained slowly, "I . . . uh, I was just thinking about you, and I got the urge to call. I hope you don't mind."

"No, I'm—it's great to hear from you," he said. "I was just thinking about you, too."

She let out her breath in relief. "You were thinking about me? I know it's been over a year since I last saw you down at the supermarket, but I think about you a lot—"

A sudden urge rushed up from his core, and he felt more at ease around her than he'd ever felt before. "That's cool," he said. "We should hang out together."

He tried to think of a nice romantic restaurant that she might like, but she beat him to the punch. "I can be there in fifteen minutes," she said, her voice thick with desire.

"Uh," he wondered at that. He hadn't been hinting at anything so intimate, but his father was out of town on a business trip and wouldn't be back for ten days, not until Christmas. If she came over, no one would be the wiser.

He glanced out the window, saw fat flakes still dropping from the sky. "Drive safely," he warned. "There's a storm outside."

He hung up. The pixie wriggled between his fingers and flapped its wings. The blue veins in its wings grew bright, and the yellow spots glowed like a tiger's knowing eyes.

"Now," the pixie said, "I'll be on my way and leave you two lovebirds to go at it. Have a happy life."

"But what if I have a question," Kerry asked. "What's your name?"

The pixie shuddered. "So you can summon me and force me to do your bidding, as if we were friends? No! I've done as you asked, now set me free!"

Dumbfounded, Kerry dropped the pixie and it swept upward and landed on the windowsill. It straightened its tunic casually and said, "That was some fine whiskey you left for me. I'd appreciate a nightcap like that on occasion, if you want to ensure my favor. Forget the milk. Just give it to me straight."

"Uh, thank you," Kerry said, unsure what to say.

"It's not as if I earned my keep," the pixie answered. "The girl has been half-mad about you for years. I just gave her a little nudge, so she'd give you that special kind of love." The pixie pierced him with a hard gaze. "But spells like this, they leave a girl... broken, if you know what I mean? So take good care of her, you hear?"

The pixie flew through the crack in the back door and whisked out over the countryside, its bright wings a cerulean blur as it weaved between fat snowflakes and winged into the Douglas fir trees up the hill.

Delilah arrived in twelve minutes flat, and when Kerry answered the door, she grabbed him tightly and clung to him with her whole body as she laid a kiss on him. He'd never been embraced so completely, and he found that every muscle relaxed at her touch. They kissed nervously at first, but it felt to Kerry that he had known her forever—they had been close in high school—and so he took her into the living room and they talked for hours, old friends, hoping to strike up something new.

He tried to be a gentleman, keep things platonic for a while at least, but as they cuddled on the couch, Delilah asked, "Why didn't you call. I've been waiting—for what—two years? God, I feel so stupid."

Kerry wondered at that. Two years? Had she really wanted a relationship that long? And what of the pixie? Had it really changed anything? "Two years?"

"Yeah, since our last date."

Our date? He didn't recall any date. Then it hit him. He'd taken her to a forgettable sci-fi movie. He'd been too shy to try to touch her, to kiss her, and afterward he'd felt like a fool.

"I remember that," he said. "I remember wanting to kiss you."

Delilah had a pretty face, a strong chin. Her lower lip trembled. "I wish you would have. I wanted you to kiss me. I would have liked it even better if you'd touched me."

She took his hand, squeezed it, and placed it on her waist, then shifted into him as if to kiss, but she held back a little.

"Sometimes," she whispered, "I get so lonely, it feels like every muscle is aching. My heart, my lips, my thighs."

She fell silent and waited for him to respond, waiting for him to touch her, to agree. They were both lonely, and only by coming together could they find a cure.

He kissed her then, and she began fumbling to take off his clothes.

It wasn't until early afternoon, when he woke up with eyes bleary and his head spinning from lack of sleep that he realized that he had forgotten all about his finals. He'd been so enamored with exploring Delilah's naked body, he missed his human anatomy final altogether.

They married two days later and the honeymoon lasted until his dad came home. His father merely grunted in acknowledgement when he met Delilah, as if worried that both of them might be rushing into a relationship. But his father was gone two days after Christmas.

He left Kerry the keys to the house and explained that he wouldn't be back. "I hardly use this place anymore. You need it more than I do. But call me whenever you want."

So Kerry began to grow bloated on unconditional love. He went into his honeymoon period even harder after Christmas, just coasting through life, and by February his grades were so low, Kerry went to the registrar's office and dropped out of college.

One dream quashed. Since student loans were his only form of support, he called his dad and got a job at the local paint retailer, with the dubious title of "Assistant Sale Manager." He'd have to travel a lot, talking with corporate clients.

Delilah didn't seem to mind. "We don't need much money. I'll be happy so long as I have you," she consoled him, and proved it with the best non-honeymoon night of his life.

In August, while he was away on a sales trip in Connecticut, Delilah gave birth to Keanu, their firstborn, and Kerry began to stress. He worried about money as he pushed his clients to make bigger purchases. Most of them were apartment-complex managers who only needed to paint every two years, and they just wanted something neutral that would keep the place looking livable. If he'd only sold paint in the colors of almond and egg-shell, he'd have done fine. No one ever ordered hot pinks or lime.

"Hey, have I got a deal for you!" became his mantra, and he'd try to keep the desperation out of his voice as he spoke on the phone. Sometimes he succeeded in wringing a little blood out of the turnips, but more often his customers just quit answering his calls.

He began to console himself with doughnuts and Mountain Dew. He told himself that it was just to keep his energy up. But the fatter he got, the more impossible it became to keep his energy up. He soon tipped the scales at 260, a lot for his small frame.

He felt like a blob, and one day when he got home and rested in his recliner, watching women on some workout channel, he told Delilah, "I think it's time I go to the gym."

Delilah merely smiled at him in that dazed manner she got, where her brown eyes went unfocused and she seemed to speak as if she were a million miles away. With her face slack, she said, "It's okay, Sweetie. There's just more of you to love."

That look in her eye, it pained him. She looked mental. His great grandfather had stroked out when he was a child, and Kerry remembered his slurred speech, his staggering. Some part of grandpa's brain had been dead, and when Kerry looked at Delilah, he knew that something inside her was gone, too. She was broken.

She sat on the edge of the recliner and cuddled gratefully while little Keanu scooted on the floor. With her ribs pressed against him, Kerry felt as if Delilah were growing thinner. Sales were down, so she had taken a part-time job at a Burger King to make up for lost money. He could smell french-fries on her work uniform, and cooking grease in her hair. He peered into her heart-shaped face, and her soft brown eyes gazed into his knowingly, almost as if she could see his guilt but didn't dare say anything about it.

I'm sorry, he wanted to say. Any sane woman would have done like his mother—nagged him to get a better job or work harder or finish college or go to the gym. Instead, Delilah busied herself constantly with fixing things around the house, mending clothes, and cutting coupons out of the newspaper. Anything to help him. Anything to save money.

He kissed her passionately. For more than a year now he had known what it felt like to be loved, truly loved, and he also realized that he didn't really know how to love her in return. So he decided to make up for it, try to be the man she deserved.

"Let's go out tonight," he offered. "Me and you. Let's go someplace special—after I get back from the gym."

So he took her out to a fine restaurant that night, and they celebrated with a bit of slow dancing.

He hoped that she understood, that she felt as loved as he did, but when he woke at three in the morning, he heard her crying in the master bathroom. He went in and found her curled into a fetal position in the shower, with all of her clothes on, and he put his arms around her and just knelt beside her.

"What's wrong?" he begged.

"That was the best date ever," she apologized. "I—I, I just can't believe how much you love me, how sweet you are. I don't feel worthy—"

"So you're crying because you're happy?" he asked.

She nodded enthusiastically. "Yes," she urged. "I thought I loved you, but now I feel it a hundred times more. And I promise, I promise, I'll be a better wife!"

Kerry felt shell-shocked. By trying to be worthy of her devotion, he realized that he would only make matters worse. She'd kill herself trying to serve him.

"Listen to me," he urged. "You're perfect just the way you are!"

Delilah shook her head and trembled as more tears flowed. He scooped her off the floor and carried her to bed, hoping to convince her of his love.

Kerry began taking more business trips in order to make more money—flying to California one week and Connecticut the next. Staying in cheap motels and hounding clients to the point that when he saw a person on the street, he no longer saw them as people—just potential sales.

On the rare days when he came home to the green hills of Oregon, he made sure to put a little whiskey in the cat's bowl, even though Maleficent had died in midwinter.

He began working out, running countless miles on the treadmill at the gym, and began to lose weight. He pumped iron and experimented with kickboxing and keto diets. But he still felt like a slob. A strong slob with a hell of kick, but a slob nonetheless.

When he was home, he tried to make up for his absence by paying attention to his wife and child, but it wore him to the bone. He didn't dare try to be mean to her, to make her love him less. Nor could he ask her to love him more. Finding the balance was emotionally exhausting.

He began to look forward to business trips, to his nights away from Delilah, away from his guilt.

He began searching through books on how to deal with the fey, but really found nothing that could help. Sometimes he wondered if he had gone insane and merely hallucinated the pixie. In fact, it seemed that at times the memories purposely slipped away, as if someone wanted him to forget what had happened.

Yet Delilah loved him and lived to serve him. She would urge him to sit in his recliner in front of the television when he got home from work, feeding him and trying to meet his every need.

Hell, sometimes he thought that she would breathe for him and digest his food for him if he asked it of her, and he despaired of finding a way to… resolve the relationship.

When he was trim enough so that an apartment manager in Florida made a pass at him, he bedded her.

She was a hot little Cubana with a gorgeous face and charming dimples.

He'd never imagined himself cheating, but somehow it felt good. For a few moments he dared wonder what Delilah would think when she found out about it, but then he jumped on the woman and screwed her again.

When he returned home that Saturday morning, he could hardly look Delilah in the eye. She had grown scrappy over the past few months, her dirty blonde hair cut into a pageboy, and she peered at him with those brown eyes as if she knew. He thought that she was so broken, she wouldn't even be able to confront him, but he was wrong.

"What did you do?" she demanded softly. Then she just gazed at him, eyes brimming with tears. But her eyes were so freaking strange: he couldn't tell if they were tears of betrayal or adoration.

"Nothing," he finally said. He lied, and she just stared at him knowingly, chewing her lower lip, and he wanted to crawl under a rock.

I wish I were dead.

He considered suicide, seriously, over the next two weeks. He deserved to die. Delilah deserved something better than him. But he also began to worry for her. There was something broken inside her, and he doubted she would ever be right in the head. She needed him to take care of her.

As penance, he dropped his client in Florida. For a few days she left him alone, but suddenly after a month she began to call his office phone at every opportunity. Finally after ten weeks he answered, "Maria—"

She roared at him, "What the hell do you want me to do with the babies!" she shouted. He just stared at her number on the phone. "The doctor says it's twins! I'm Catholic. I can't just abort them."

Kerry was Catholic, too, sort of. He couldn't ask her to abort the babies. But he couldn't really afford to do anything else.

That night at dinner, while roasted salmon and asparagus steamed on the table, he stared at Delilah as she spoon-fed the baby. For a long time he just watched her.

Until she gazed at him with a firm jaw and demanded, "What did you do?" She'd been waiting for him to get ready to confess. He saw it in her demeanor. She'd waited those ten weeks. There was understanding in that question, and damnation and forgiveness. He could hear the undertone, "I love you unconditionally. I'll love you forever. Just tell me the goddamned truth!"

So he told her. "I made love to another woman. She's going to have twins. She wants me to pay child support, and I don't know what to do."

Delilah gasped as if he had just shoved a spear through her heart. Her mouth formed an 'O' of grief that seemed to stretch her jaw to the breaking point. "Oh, damn you!" she wailed.

She pulled the baby out of the highchair, raced to the baby's room, and began to clean out the baby's dresser.

He went to the bedroom door and begged, "I'm sorry. Please, forgive me. I'll never do anything like that again."

Delilah didn't answer. She put Keanu on the bed and stripped off his dirty clothes in firm, quick jerks, as if she were shucking corn.

When she had a new outfit on the baby—complete with a coat, Delilah ran to her own room and packed her bags, and Kerry wished that she could leave—that she could find the strength to abandon him, that she would reclaim some part of her lost soul.

But he knew that it was in vain. Some part of him realized that he had been trying to drive her away, get her to hate him. Perhaps then it would break the spell.

She picked up the baby and a suitcase and stormed out of the house, and he lay down in their bedroom, the lights off, the house as dark as his soul.

But as he lay in bed near midnight, wracked with guilt, sobbing, she crawled into bed soundlessly and hugged him so tightly, she just clung. Her fingers were like meat hooks, digging into him, as if afraid that someone would try to pull them apart.

When she fell asleep an hour later, whimpering, Kerry untangled himself from her arms, went to the kitchen and poured whiskey into the old red cat bowl and set it on the back porch, then just waited in the cool night air.

The old tales said to put milk in the bowl to attract pixies, but that just attracted feral cats, raccoons, and opossums. He was after more elusive game.

He stood on the porch for long minutes, breathing the scent of hay in the fields and staring up at the night sky. A meteor flashed against a dusting of stars, and he heard a lapping noise.

Surprised, he looked down at his feet. Something had disturbed the whiskey, causing small ripples in the bowl. Yet there was nothing to be seen.

"Och," the pixie crooned, "the good stuff!"

"Hello," Kerry said softly, "old friend." He gazed down, but the pixie didn't appear. Just the porch with an old bowl on it in a wan circle of yellow light.

"Och, don't go trying to sweet-talk me," the pixie groused. "We're not friends—never were. I gave you what you wanted because you cast a curse on me, and that is all. It wasn't even a proper business transaction—more like extortion."

"I didn't mean any harm," Kerry apologized.

He heard a rustling in the wind, as if the pixie were flying away, laughing. Kerry begged, "Wait! Stop! Can you fix her?" Kerry loved his wife—realized that he'd always loved Delilah, but hadn't known how to do it proper.

He couldn't see the creature fluttering out in the dark by the lilac bushes, but he could hear its wings softly clacking.

The creature's voice arose from everywhere and nowhere, whispering in his mind. "Why should I have to do all that work just because you've decided to grow a damned conscience? I never cheated you! I gave you exactly what you demanded! You humans—you're all such damned fools!"

The sound of wings was lost in a sigh of wind, as if a cool breeze blew up from under the hill.

"I know I'm a fool," Kerry admitted, hoping to appease the creature, but the night was empty except for the sound of receding laughter.

Kerry went to the kitchen. He wasn't a drinker, had only kept a little whiskey around for the pixie. But he guzzled the last of the whiskey straight, let it burn his throat on the way down until he felt the fire in the pit of his belly.

Delilah, I was never worthy of you, he thought as the whiskey made his head spin, and wondered how he could fix things.

Yes, he could become a better man, try to live worthy of Delilah's affection, but what would that do? He shuffled to bed and carefully lay down beside her, heard her softly breathing. She cried out a bit in her sleep and grimaced, a frown of hurt in her pale face.

There is something broken in her head. Her brain was damaged, as surely as she'd stroked out.

She's not even human anymore.

And that is when he recognized the depth of his betrayal. He'd turned her into a puppet. Something doomed to love him in spite of himself.

There is a place in the human heart so dark, that the thought of dying seems like wisdom, a sort of escape.

In his bathroom medicine cabinet Kerry kept some sleeping pills, the ones he used after long flights when he really needed some rest. The note on the bottle warned him not to mix the pills with alcohol.

He went into the master bathroom, checked the bottle, and found that it was nearly full. He dry-swallowed all thirty-six.

It will be okay, he told himself. I have enough life insurance so that she should be able to get a fresh start, and soon she'll be free of me.

He stumbled back to bed, and collapsed by her side, hoping for some sleep. He realized that he hadn't had a good night's sleep in nearly two years, and now looked forward to it, even if he never woke.

"I'm done," he said, and his mind seemed to fall into a spiral so that he was spinning down, down.

The night crawled on and Kerry's body grew cool to the touch, then began to stiffen.

Delilah half-woke from her sleep and snuggled closer, felt how cold her "cuddly bear" was—so cold that it seemed he could have frozen to death.

With a start she lurched into a sitting position, her heart hammering, and felt his face to be certain. There was no warmth to his touch, and he was so cold and stiff. She had to wonder what had happened. A heart attack, at 22?

She felt that she was falling, falling, being sucked toward death with him. She couldn't imagine how she would survive without him. Will my heart go on beating? Would I even want it to?

No. She wouldn't. She grabbed Kerry around the shoulders, sobbed, and kissed his cold lips, somehow hoping he would come back to life. She smelled the whiskey on his breath and wondered at it, for she'd never known him to drink.

Kerry's lips were parted, his face as bloodless as snow. His fine auburn hair was a halo in the starlight that beamed through the window. She clung harder, listened for his breathing, and put her ear to his chest. She clung to his shoulders, and just lay there, willing him back to life.

She wondered if she should call 911, but realized that if she did, the authorities will come take him from me.

I couldn't bear that.

She wanted to keep him forever, make him hers, and so she just lay next to him and held on for dear life and whispered over and over, "It will be okay, Baby. It will be all right. I love you just the way you are."

# Time to Play

AJ Benson

At the base of the mountain, torchlight flickered in a cave opening, piercing the starless night, beckoning. A lonely raven cawed, and Kallon's heart raced in anticipation. He was certain this cave held the next artifact, map, or talisman he needed. Hiding by a large pine tree, his well-muscled Dwarvish legs ached from the long night behind him, and his mind raced with the long day ahead.

This cave was only an objective in his greater quest: get to the Lunasee Waterfalls on the far side of the Arbourre Hills—claim the power that came with the dragon's eye gem he would find there—then avenge his father's death and restore honor to his clan. He only had to do it before the other ninety-eight warriors on the quest, including the three dwarves sleeping by a dwindling campfire between Kallon and the cave.

Kallon enabled stealth-mode on his armor and the metal plates silenced. He looked to make certain the armor had dulled appropriately, avoiding any reflections from the torchlight or campfire, and slid from behind towering pine. The campfire crackled, and one of the dwarves flailed his arm about, as if shooing mosquitoes. Another, mumbling about bees, twitched and jerked in his sleep. The third rolled over, almost causing Kallon to tumble into the orange embers of the dying fire.

A piercing voice, not of this world, interrupted Kallon's treacherous footsteps. "Mika, I told you to get off that game and take out the trash an hour ago!"

Irritated, Mika glanced at his mom, who was standing, hands on her hips, just on the other side of the living room. "Take off the earphones." Her lips were pursed in agitation.

Mika paused the video game and uncovered one of his ears. "I *heard* you. I'll get to it." *I've already cleaned my room, put away laundry, cleaned the bathroom, and made my own birthday cake. Let me sit here for just a minute.*

In a calmer but insistent voice, his mom continued, "Your grandparents will be here in an hour, and the trash still needs to go out."

"I'm about to finish up, Mom." His deep voice carried across the living room like a chasm. "Five more minutes."

She walked out of the room, and Mika covered his ear again. *Since I'm paused, might as well get Kallon more armor.* He went to the equipment page and added some chainmail to Kallon's medieval garb. *Why doesn't real life have a pause button?* Mika ran his hand through his unkempt hair and returned to the game, epic music swelling. A message flashed from the game, a birthday present. Opening it, he discovered a claymore sword, inscribed with futhark runes, that caused twice the damage of his old sword. *Dope.*

Freshly equipped, Kallon made his way to the cave opening. The walls were cold and wet. Every ten feet were iron sconces holding torches, and the warm flicker pulled him farther and higher into the cave. As the floor leveled, the tunnel opened into a chamber that was reminiscent more of a palace than a cave. Light came from the wall sconces and a white taper candle on a large oak, lion claw-footed desk. Gone was the cold damp, replaced by warm dry air, and Kallon ran his hand along a polished wall as he stepped onto a lush red carpet spread across the chamber.

From behind the large oak desk, a hefty man, perhaps a half-giant, jumped up and rushed at Kallon. The man screamed in an unknown language and lashed out with a long sword. Kallon dodged the first blow, struck the man's left arm, causing him to curse as deep-red blood soaked his sleeve. Kallon rolled to the left. The man extended his reach for a piercing jab that scraped off

Kallon's armor. With his opponent off-balance from the botched strike, Kallon swung out with his claymore—

A high-pitched voice interrupted the battle.

"Mika, I said take the trash out."

Mika glanced at his mom, who was again in the entrance to the hall. He pulled off one earphone, and then looked back at his laptop. In the interruption, Kallon had taken a serious blow and fallen to the ground. Glowering, the stranger now stood over Kallon. Mika paused the game.

"Mom, you made me lose most of my health!"

His mom closed her eyes and shook her head. "This get-together is for *your* birthday!" She strode down the hall, her coral-pink shirt disappearing from sight like the sun setting in fast-forward.

"Why won't she get off my case? I said I'll do it," Mika muttered under his breath and focused again on his game.

Kallon pulled a dagger from his hip pocket and with one quick motion, nailed the man's foot to the floor. The man howled like a hellhound. Kallon jumped to his feet, he engaged the runes on his new sword and swung. The fighter turned to smoke as his hit points plummeted to zero. Kallon sheathed his sword, wincing at the sound of fingernails on a chalkboard as the blade slid into its scabbard.

He scanned the room. It was empty except for the desk, an ornate wooden chair, a small black-lacquered jewelry box, and a coffee-colored bookshelf filled with books.

Mika noticed four choices for Kallon on his screen:

`Open the box.`

`Check out the books.`

`Open the desk.`

`Leave the cave.`

*Always explore before leaving.*

Kallon unlatched the lacquered box. Inside were three items: a bronze skeleton key, a small pocket-watch made of iron, and a dozen silver coins. He collected all of them. The coins jingled softly as he slipped them in his pouch.

On the bookshelf were almost two dozen books, covered in cloths from blood-red to sky-blue and in various degrees of wear-and-tear. *Ancient of Ages* by Morgana Tyr Rani Avery, *100 Years of Apothecary* by Molly O. Philis, *The Power of Time* by Bane Athan Alberic Lefey, and *Mirror Mirror* by Voler Lenfant were all on the top shelf. Kallon ran his fingers silently along the titles on the second shelf where *Minutes of Magic* by Bohgus Alexander Ambrose Liegend lay open. Kallon picked it up, and the sound of flipping pages momentarily flooded his senses. It seemed to be a spell book. He set it back on the narrow shelf, dust particles floating like glitter into the air.

Kallon opened the desk drawer with a creak. Only a parchment scroll, a raven-feather quill, and a bottle of, what Kallon hoped was, maroon ink were tucked inside. He carefully opened the scroll and winced as it crackled, several small pieces of parchment drifting onto the plush carpet. It was an invitation to visit the castle near Lunasee from someone named BAAL. As Kallon set it back in the desk and closed the drawer with a scrape, he sensed he was being watched.

A nasally voice from the kitchen pierced into Mika's thoughts. "Mika, the trash. It's been twenty minutes already."

Not daring enough to say it out loud, Mika vented silently about his mom by typing words into the chat window: leave me alone!

A raspy male voice responded into his headset. "Yeh can make 'er do that." Mika looked at the screen. At the opening of the cave was a tall figure, cloaked in black. His hair was jet black, and his eyes equally so. A raven perched on his shoulder.

"Mika Bryan Watson, get off that game!"

The raven swooped past Kallon again and the cloaked figure continued in his brogue. "It's possible. Yeh can get 'er to leave yeh alone. I'll show yeh how."

Mika typed into the chat: `wasnt talking about the raven`

The stranger replied, "Nor was I."

Mika furrowed his brow.

The cloaked man continued, "Let me show yeh. What can it hurt? If yeh don't want to continue, jes' quit de game."

*Quit the game? Dude, you broke the 4th wall. That's messed up.* Glancing at the unlit hallway, Mika typed: `sure. what do I need to do?`

"Yeh're already on yer way. This quest will bring yeh powers in addition to those of the dragon's eye. On yer way to Lunasee to get de dragon's eye, yeh will need to build a few skills and stop at Noegnud Castle to set free a warrior. Dat is all I ask. His help will save yeh time and ensure yeh get to de dragon's eye first." The sconced torches flickered.

Mika hovered the mouse above the character. Epic-movie music played into his headset. The pop-up box identified the stranger as "Author of the Scroll, mysterious stranger, a fey." The character had crazy hit points, but low armor class. Choices appeared in the lower right corner.

`Go with the stranger.`

`Continue alone.`

`Fight him.`

"Mika!" his mom called again. Mika's lip curled in agitation.

The mysterious stranger waved at Kallon to follow. Mika selected number one, and Kallon strode to the cave entrance. Three wisps of smoke hovered where the sleeping dwarves had been as Kallon and the fey continued towards Lunasee falls.

Once in a while, the fey's raspy voice broke the monotony of leather boots marching over dead leaves to praise Kallon's skill. In an ambush, Kallon killed several warriors and looted some jewels, a pair of daggers, an ash wand with a citrine crystal in its filigreed handle, and a book of magic, which was indecipherable. In the back of the book was a list of random names written in a hurried scribble: Vondal Gamir, Lillian Mall, L. Yellowleaf, John Mether, and dozens of others. The fey asked to see the spell book, which Kallon allowed, but when Kallon offered the wand, the fey put his hand up to decline. The raven cawed.

"We haven't time to play, Kallon. We must retrieve someting more precious than any of dese. We have important matters to discuss as we walk. Yeh have demonstrated yer skill, and yer interest in changing how things work. I have very powerful magic, and yeh could have it too. Yeh jes have to help me out. Even now, yeh are only one successful task away from having de power to slow time. De more kills yeh get, de more control yeh have over time, and de more magic that comes into existence. Ready to give it a try, Kallon?"

Kallon nodded.

"Good. Dere is a small village ahead of us. Dey have a few fighters but are mostly farmers. It should be easy for a dwarf of yer skill. If yeh can take out all of de fighters, I shall gift yeh."

As they broke the crest of the hill, Kallon went to work, slicing down villagers and looting their bodies. However, the villagers turned fierce, screaming and swinging axes, when he killed a woman coming out of the ancient temple of Dileb, God of the Fields, Mika heard a rapid beeping in the head set and realized Kallon's health was at half a heart, and the dwarf was forced to retreat.

The fey appeared next to him as out of nowhere. "Dat was an unfortunate loss, Kallon. But I have confidence in yeh. Perhaps yeh should light the roofs on fire. Dey are made of straw. It should be easy enough for yeh. If yeh succeed, I will grant yeh not only de ability to slow time but to speed it up."

An increasingly frustrated voice called from the kitchen, "Mika!" Mika paused the game and, ignoring his mom, decided to tip the odds in his favor. He uploaded a cheat mod to keep his health auto-replenished. He was able to find it, typed his username `M-I-K-A-3-5`, and upload it quickly enough.

Kallon agreed to the stranger's offer. Mika smiled, knowing he had tipped the odds in Kallon's favor. The dwarf easily destroyed the village by lighting a mere two roofs on fire, taking no damage himself. The dwarf returned to the hilltop from which the fey watched, admiring the flames leaping from one house to another like toads along the river. The fey tsk'd at Kallon, though, and shook his head. "Well done, but we have a wee problem." The screen pixelated.

Mika muttered under his breath as he tapped *Escape* and then returned to the game, hoping the problem would stop. It pixelated again. "Ugh. Stupid glitch."

"It's no glitch. Yeh cheated. While I love ingenuity and drive, cheatin' was not part of the deal."

Mika sucked in his breath and typed into the chat window.

can you hear me? and what are you talking about?

"Yeh know what I'm talkin' about, Mika. Yeh uploaded a cheat mod. *Dat* was not part of the deal."

*How does a character know my real name? WTH? Did they program that in? Ah, my username.*

The fey continued, "Now, to be able to unlock de magic, yeh need Kallon to solve a wee mystery in addition to freeing de warrior. I like yeh, Mika, and I am confident yeh can do this. Past the bend in the river is Noegnud. Dere yeh will find a warrior trapped in a dungeon. Free him and solve the mystery, and I will unlock not only yer ability to slow and speed time, but to pause it as well. Yeh could play video games as long as yeh want, and yeh would never have to worry about being nagged ag'in."

Kallon went with the fey. They waded through the waist-high river. As they climbed the banks on the far side, a small stone structure came into view. The fey took Kallon by the elbow. "De person yeh must save is down these steps and to the left."

An increasingly frustrated voice called to Mika from the kitchen. "Pleeeease take out the trash!"

The fey whispered seductively, "Hurry. De sooner yeh release him, de sooner yeh get yer freedom from 'er naggin'."

Kallon made his way down the steps, ash wand at the ready, citrine glowing. The walls deadened all outside sounds. At the bottom of the steps was a dark cell with iron bars. The fey motioned in silence for him to push open the door.

Kallon was given two game options:

`Do you refuse?`

`Do you enter in silence?`

Mika chose the second option, and the door gave way with a long creak. There was old straw on the floor, a water-filled bucket, and a bench visible in the dim citrine light. Kallon stepped in, walking toward the dark corner where the prisoner must be. *Why did he stay here if the door was unlocked?* The door clanked hard behind him. The fey laughed as he removed his hood.

Kallon banged on the cell door, as he yelled in a booming voice that reverberated across the cells. "You tricked me! What do you want?"

The fey smirked in the pale-yellow light from Kallon's wand. "Of course, I tricked yeh. What? Yeh tink power doesn't come at a cost? Yeh have to provide yer energy to me, and in turn, I will gift yeh the power of time. De fey used to take babies, but times have changed and now we work wit' teenage boys. Yeh have so much more angst dan an infant can generate, Mika. De fey have controlled time for two millennia. We are willing to gift yeh power in return fer yer angst. Dere is a catch for us. Yeh must choose to play our game, willingly. Revenge of the Clans is a game yeh're very good at, Mika. Yeh might even be good enough to receive even greater powers in de world *outside* de game."

Mika growled into the gaming headset. "I'm not playing your stupid game anymore." He began to take off his headset.

"Yeh may not want to do that. Look towards the kitchen, Mika." His mother stood motionless in the doorway, frozen, holding a piece of lasagna. The scent of oregano wafted in his direction.

Mika could not control the panic in his voice. "What have you done to her? How the… How did you know I was taking off my headset?"

"Well, I'm glad to have yer attention. To release 'er, yeh must agree to continue to play. It's really quite simple, yeh see."

Fear clouded Mika's thoughts. He saw no other option. "How do I get out?"

"Yeh have someting in yer possession that will get yeh out, but yeh need to figure dat out fer yerself. *Dat* is the mystery. I will be waiting at the top of the steps. Yeh have all de time in de world." He cackled and ascended the steps, and Kallon was left in the yellow glow of his wand.

Kallon pulled out his sack and emptied it of its contents, coins jingling as they hit the floor. The citrine on the end of the wand seemed to have little sparks of energy running through it. He tried the skeleton key and several opening spells with the wand, but none worked. There was the book that he couldn't read, silver pieces, a moonstone—usually good luck for nighttime adventures and travelers, the pocket-watch, and daggers. None of the items seemed suited for the task.

Mika attempted to get choices to pop up for Kallon, but the text on the screen merely read: `Typed commands only.` Mika tried numerous commands, and Kallon tried to open the door with brute strength.

"It doesn't work that way," came a weak, gravelly voice from across the cell. Kallon had forgotten about the prisoner. "You need a traveler's talisman to open the door." Kallon looked at the moonstone in his hand. As he held it near the door, it illuminated like a glow stick on Halloween.

"Who are you?" Mika asked through his headset.

"I'm Ricky. From the real world. St. Clair, Michigan to be specific. I wish I had not been so stupid."

Mika lifted his eyes in the real world, looked at his mom, and his heart ached. He wished she would move, even to yell at him, and could almost hear her voice, "Mika Bryan Watson, get off that game now!" Whenever she used his full name, he knew he had better do what she had told him to do. Awareness dawned. *That's it!*

Ricky continued, "I took out the fey who brought me here, a fey named John, but his companion quickly bound me to this cell. I am stuck in this dungeon until another warrior frees me. I don't know how long it has been, but when they can stop time, I am not sure it matters. Maybe you can take him out and we can both go home."

"Ricky, I don't know his name."

"He had to tell you during the quest. That's one of the rules. He had to provide a way out. *Think.*"

"Wait, the fey you took out was named John?" Kallon grabbed the spell book from his sack and flipped to the back. *Vondal A. Gamir, Lillian Mall, L. Yellowleaf, John Mether…* "John Mether?"

The prisoner stood in excitement and came over to where Kallon was holding the book. "That's it!"

"Do you think his name might be Vondal, Lillian…"

Ricky shook his dirty-blond, shoulder-length hair. "No. Those are the names of those already marked in this game. Think, dude. What other names?"

"Well, the character information said he was the author of the scroll which was signed BAAL, and that was an invitation to Noegnud!"

Ricky clicked his tongue. "They have more than one name. Maybe those were initials?"

"There *were* books in the cave where I met him."

"Any with authors with the initials of BAAL?"

"Yeah! Actually, there were two!"

"Quiet, dude, he's coming back." Ricky returned quietly to the darkest corner of the cell.

"I see yer moonstone glowing. So, yeh figured it out. Will we be continuin' our quest together, or will yeh rot here like Richard? I did not ferget about yeh, my friend, nor yer treachery." Ricky shifted the straw in the darkness but said nothing.

Kallon strode to the door, using the moonstone as a key. The cell door unlocked with a click. As he left the cell, he glanced in Ricky's direction. Kallon ascended the dark stairs by the light of his wand.

The fey smiled crookedly as he spoke. "I'm glad we have an agreement. De power of time will be yers, and yeh don' have to listen to 'er naggin' anymore."

Mika smiled at his mom and spoke into the headset. "Yes, I have power, but not the one you think. I know your name."

The fey stopped in his tracks. "Do yeh now, Mika? Yeh know, yeh get only one shot. Otherwise, though yeh may take me out, yeh will be imprisoned like yer friend."

"Bane Athan Alberic Lefey, you will release your hold over the time in my world."

The fey scowled. "How did yeh figure it out?"

"The scroll in your cave was signed BAAL. There were two books written by authors with those initials, though, and I had to guess whether it was *Minutes of Magic* or *The Power of Time*. Your own words gave you away. Goodbye, Bane." With that, the fey disappeared into a shadowy wisp from the game.

Kallon checked the dungeon, and Ricky had gone too, but there was a message in Mika's chat window: let me know if you need anything

It was from Richard007. Mika marked him as a friend and logged out. He wiped his sweaty palms on his jeans and looked at his mom.

She shook her head as if coming out of a fog, her blue eyes regaining their awareness. "I thought some lunch might encourage you to get off that thing for a bit."

Mika got up. "I'll take the trash out first, Mom. I should have done it a while ago. Sorry."

"I was young too, once. I get it. I'll leave lunch on the table."

Mika kissed her cheek and smiled to himself as he grabbed the trash bag and headed outside. *I'm so glad that's over. I'll delete that game after grandma and grandpa leave.*

As he approached the end of the drive, a gravelly voice spoke to him from across the street. Mika lifted his head to see a tall man wearing a black hoodie and leaning against a light post. "It's so nice that yeh help yer mom out. So many teens don' make the time to do it. Dey only make time to play." Mika glanced at the bags in his hands and back to the man, but he was no longer there.

# Promises Made, Promises Broken

Clayton Snyder

When Atlantic City ate twenty dollars of Johnny Montana's money in less time than it took to do a rail of coke in the dimly lit bathroom of the Grand, he left his stool in front of the blackjack table and stepped outside. Even at nearly midnight, the city teemed with life, a reef on the Jersey coast, people and cars flashing by like gaudy shoals, moving this way and that, schools of men and women and men and ladies of the night—because it wasn't right to call them whores, his mother always said—traveling in packs.

Sometimes they closed ranks, making it hard to get around them, slowing traffic, birthing frustration. Sometimes they split, like some deeper instinct had grabbed them by the hindbrain and throttled it, as predators lurked and stalked in their midst. Slick men with black coats and dead eyes. Expensive suits bulging in suspicious places. Teeth shining like the gold on their necks and fingers and wrists. The type of people his mother called knee-breakers, men who would just as soon as eat your liver than look at you and never blink once. Even Johnny, with only two hours into the city, had sense to stay away.

Instead, he cast about, looking for something new, something grand to see. Casinos lined the shore, marching beside the surf like Roman soldiers, a bulwark against natural beauty. The wood of the boardwalk was an anachronism beside bright neon and digital signs that hurt his eyes when they flashed and dimmed the moon to an annoyance. Even the smell of the ocean had been pushed back, bottled to the alleys facing the sea, beaten and boxed by the scents of fried dough, hot oil, and hot dogs marinated three days under water coated with an iridescent sheen.

Someone jostled his arm, and he turned to apologize—his mother said politeness was the way of the angels, and only the devil was an asshole—but they were gone. He straightened, and light, new light, fresh light, like a sign from on high, caught his eye. Across the street, a bar, two stories, white and brown, a sign clinging to its roof like a gull waiting for a dropped fry. THE CONTINENTAL, it read, but to Johnny, who'd stepped off the bus only two hours ago, his sainted mother six feet under and twelve hundred miles away, and the last fifty dollars to his name in his pocket, it felt like home.

He stepped off the curb, and into the bar. Dim light. Red velvet booths. Paneled walls. Hardwood floors stained chestnut. Duke Ellington from the battered jukebox in the corner. It reminded him of the room his father had left behind so long ago, cigar smoke and bourbon clinging to the fabric. His father, who had left on a promise and a whim. He was gonna be rich, he said. He was gonna bring them everything they ever wanted. He'd met a man who could make it happen. And then he was gone. Smoke in the wind. Johnny settled on a bench and smiled at the bartender. A couple dollars got him a whiskey-Coke. Another then, and another. The city was exciting, but this—this was orgasmic.

When he woke up three days later, Johnny did three things. He settled up his tab, which the bar had been kind enough to leave open, despite the puddle of vomit beside the jukebox. Second, he stepped outside for a breath of fresh air. He'd found joy in alcohol, in the fiery tang of whiskey and whisky, the meaty weight of beer, and the light tang of vodka, but sometimes a man just needed to peek outside to convince himself all that booze was worth it. The third thing that happened was the slow realization that he was broke in a strange city, and if he wanted to do more than bathe in the gutters, he'd need a job.

He looked across the city, painted pink and purple in the dawn light, and considered. Food vendor seemed like more work than it was worth. He doubted he could get a job as a taxi driver, having only seen the boardwalk and the bus station. He tapped his foot, and watched morning traffic come to life. A small three-wheeled cart, shaped like a rudimentary car, passed, pushed by a young man, a quiet couple inside. More joined the flow of traffic, from hotel to casino and back, never leaving the strip. He watched them go and considered. That, he could do. That he could do well.

And that was how Johnny came to live in Atlantic City for three years.

He'd seen a lot since stepping off that bus from Biloxi. Cokeheads and strippers, women dressed like schoolmarms cozied beside men in leather harnesses, men nodding in his cab, needle hanging from the inside of their elbow as he pushed them to their hundred-thousand-dollar a night hotel, bodies curled up in the alleys, clouds of flies coating the corpses like a cloak.

This though, this was something new. As his sainted mother might have said—you can't judge every book by its cover, unless it's smut, then you should throw it in the trash. The man approaching his pushcart was tall and willowy, ears tapered to somewhat of a point. His eyes were slightly elongated, tilted up at the corners, as though permanently enjoying an amusing joke. His clothing, an all-white suit, was immaculate and flattering. His skin was the black of mahogany, the fingers that clutched a slim cigarette, long, like a pianist. He smiled at Johnny.

"Fiver for a ride to the end of the row?" The accent that marked the words held a lilt.

Irish, then, Johnny supposed. He'd known a few in his day, and even more here, though they went by the names of Jameson and Guinness and Bailey. They didn't talk much, but then they didn't have to. He did most of the talking for them after an hour or two together. Luckily for this man, he'd just had a drink with one not long ago, and he was feeling magnanimous. He'd take the fare despite the lowball. He nodded, and the man climbed in.

Johnny put his shoulder to the cart, and was shocked when it shot forward, as though the man weighed nothing. He paused and uttered an apology.

"Sorry 'bout that. Must be stronger than I look."

The man chuckled from the cab and peered around the side. "You're a funny lad. Tell you what. You take me to the end of the block, and I'll multiply the pay one hundred percent."

Five hundred dollars for a trip to the end of the block? He didn't believe it, and said as much.

"You're screwing with me. But tell you what, I'll take you, because even a slow night is better than no night. Then you pay me the five, and we'll go each our own."

The man pulled out a money clip, and snapped off five crisp hundreds. He fanned them.

"End of the block."

Johnny swallowed, wished his friend Jameson was there. He stared at the cash, and thought about all the friends it would buy him. He set his jaw and nodded.

"Sit back sir. I'll get you there." He would, too.

And the sooner the better. He'd had passengers like this before. Liked to play games. Predators smelling blood in the water. Better done, better gone, his mother would say. The stranger dropped back into the cab, and Johnny leaned his shoulder into the cart, legs digging in. It rolled forward, easy, but not as before. He set a steady pace. Sooner done, sooner gone.

Sweat beaded his forehead though the ocean breeze, cool and sweet, wicked it away almost as quickly, and he was grateful for it. Even off the Atlantic, the summer heat could burn a man up like a short match. Time passed with what felt to Johnny like the second coming of a glacial age. The world fell into silence, even the ever-present cries of greedy gulls fading. The quiet rushed into his ears, halting his progress. He looked up, then behind. The Continental was a small white blotch behind him, the details fuzzed like an oil painting. Ahead, a lake mirrored the sky, and at its far side, a wide forest. Here, Johnny stood on the high slope of a mountainside, though the boardwalk still crept and curled across the landscape, a road for his passenger.

His heart hammered in fear, and he stepped back, letting the cart sit.

"Everything okay?" his passenger called.

"No. Not in the least," Johnny said.

He sat, feeling the cool hard boards beneath the backs of his thighs. Maybe that last drink had done him. Three years pickling his liver. Did he think it wouldn't reach his brain? Like it lived in a gated community, safe from the depredations of a broken world? He snorted in anger and shame, and threw a rock, watching it arc down the mountainside.

Is that something that would happen in a hallucination?

"Tempus fugit," the man said from the cart. "Did you know we invented that saying? Five years, five hundred—what's time when you're immortal?"

Johnny frowned at the cart. If the world was this, what was that?

"Regardless," the man said. "Five hundred. End of the block." A dark hand pointed toward the forest below. "Just a bit further. And if you can't, well. There are others perhaps more capable. Though the journey back is longer than the way forward, and your lives are so short. Fireflies in a winter storm."

He reached his hand from the side of the cab, and Johnny saw a glow to it, a sheen that highlighted the fine bones, the elegant nails. The passenger made a flicking motion, like discarding trash. Johnny looked back, at the smudge of the Continental, then forward, to the lake and the forest. He sighed, once, deep and heavy.

"Screw it," he said.

His mother had once said there are some journeys that can only be finished by going forward, no matter the pain inherent in them. Even if it felt like knives in your legs, you moved forward, because going backwards would be throwing away all you'd suffered.

He pushed to his feet, and once again put his shoulder against the cart. They moved. Again, time slipped by, and he thought that maybe he'd be here forever, Sisyphus shoving a passenger car. But no, he was making headway. Soon, the water was beside him, lapping at the boards. The sound made him thirsty. It made him think of amber liquid, and the burn that followed. It made him think of the way, when he had just the right amount, butterflies lit in his brain, and unicorns shat rainbows in his heart.

Then the smell of something long dead and bloated came to him, floating and rolling on the gentle tide. Pale flesh, bloated and wrapped in algae. The skin of the skull had swollen around a crown, tarnished and iron. The face, mottled and distended and fly-bitten, was familiar to Johnny. The scent was like nothing he'd experienced before, but not unlike a deer he'd once found in the woods, crawling with maggots in the June sun.

"You know him," the man said, unprompted. "He once came to us from a far-off place, hoping to gain. To use. But time is not gentle, and neither are we."

Johnny's stomach clenched, and he turned his head, shoving as hard as possible. He stuffed the memory away, folded and hidden in a corner of his mind so he could take it out later. Tears threatened to come, but his anger forced them back first, and then rationale. The world was broken, just as promises were. This would not change the path he had taken. Perhaps though, given time and inspection, it would change the path he walked? He shook his head to clear the thoughts and moved on.

The lake sped by. They slipped into the shadow of the forest, the scents of conifer and mulch replacing that of corruption. Johnny breathed easy again, slowed his pace. Ahead, the boardwalk ended. Here, sunlight speared between leaf and bough in shafts that dazzled his eyes. Small animals scampered and played in the undergrowth, and larger skulked in the shadows. The cart rolled to a halt, and Johnny heard the sound of bootheels on wood. He waited, but no one came to the other side to pay him. Anger at being stiffed overtook fear, and Johnny stepped around the side, to check the seat and look for his passenger. Ahead, the city stretched out before him, and the crowds once again swept across the concrete.

Johnny snapped a look backwards, but again found only city. He cast one forlorn look at the seat, finding only faded threadbare cloth, worn by passenger and sun. He climbed in and leaned back, closing his eyes. It'd been a long day. A hard day. He needed a drink, but the sight of his father roiling in the surf punched into his skull, and he thought maybe water would do for now. After a moment, he chuckled to himself, his dear departed mother's voice echoing in his head.

A man who trusts carefully can never be made a fool, she'd say, but it's a fool who trusts promises anyway.

# The Concert Chaperone Conspiracy

David Boop

Reginald Dallas hated lines, thinking the necessity was really the whole world conspiring against his schedule.

Hours wasted in traffic.

Endless lines at the grocery.

Even waiting to take a piss at the bar tempted the bodyguard to pull his gun and clear the rabble.

The line he stood in with his goddaughter, Eryn Perlis, ranked as the worst. They, as well as a few hundred others, waited to enter the concert Eryn had "dreamed about all her life." Well, if fourteen years was a lifetime, then waiting for this concert felt like two for Reggie.

But then he could never tell her no, could he?

*Please, Uncle Reggie! It's all I want for my birthday. No money. I just want to see him in person!*

Eryn had sent him a link to the fan club's web site for buying pre-release, premium tickets; VIP tickets that—surprise, surprise—didn't include VIP treatment. Thus, their sojourn with the rabble.

The theater pushed back against the encroaching night with brilliant billboards and dual spotlights that traced the clouds like swords dueling in the sky. Booths for corporate sponsors hawked energy drinks, sunscreen and worthless trinkets along the front.

Reggie warned Eryn that concerts were too dangerous for her to attend, and maintaining security around her would be next to impossible. Being Eryn's godfather came second to his job as her protector; a role she made difficult. Keeping tabs on a normal fourteen-year-old girl was hard enough, but her father, Landry

Perlis, had secrets; the type of secrets that came with ready-made enemies for him…and his daughter.

As if that wasn't enough, in the last few months Eryn had lost most of the gangliness that went with mid-puberty, morphing her into the spitting image of her mother, Kynzie: almond-shaped face, long platinum tresses and the lithe body men started wars over.

At least, they had for Kynzie.

"Thank you, Uncle Reggie." Eryn bumped her shoulder against his—the in-public version of a hug.

"Yeah, sure. No problem."

"You probably don't think I appreciate what you do for me. I do."

Reggie mumbled, "It's my duty *and* my pleasure."

Eryn giggled, and he blushed.

"You did stuff for my mom, too, didn't you? Bodyguard stuff. And more."

That came out of left field. Usually, if she had questions about her mom, she went to Landry.

"Sometimes."

"Bad things?"

"Sometimes. That was my job. Doing bad things so good people stay good." He raised an eyebrow at her. "Where is all this coming from?"

Eryn blushed that time. "I overheard the kitchen staff talking. That you and Mom were close, really close, but Dad never seemed to mind. Never got, like, jealous or anything. Made me wonder some things."

"That's because your father knew I would die before I'd let your mother get hurt, even by me."

"What was she like? And I don't want the candy-coated version."

Reggie looked around. This line of questioning made him uncomfortable. "Can we change the subject? When did you start liking this type of music?"

Eryn shrugged. "I dunno. All of sudden. His music started speaking to me, like he knew my most secret feelings. He's all the rage around school. Well, the boys don't like him, not the straight ones anyway, 'cause the girls think he's so hot."

The dreamy way she said "hot" made Reggie uneasy. He didn't know what would be was worse; explaining what some of the lyrics the wanna-be Jagger meant, or realizing she already knew?

Kynzie's bluntness had brought on the same awkwardness he felt in that moment. Reggie's complete discretion had earned him the place as her most trusted friend. She accepted Reggie as family despite the smell of blood on his hands he could never quite rinse away.

Without warning, a radio station's van blared the band's music over the waiting crowd and nearly blew out Reggie's eardrums. The energy of the crowd spiked.

*As if we won't hear enough of it inside?*

Reggie's tolerance for overly-theatrical, post-grunge wore thin. At his age, he'd heard it all, and the current trend in themed albums harkened to the Seventies progressive rock—which, in itself, was just a shout-out to operatic works of Schubert and Beethoven.

Nothing was original.

"Shaina! Tegan!"

Dropped at the curb, Eryn's prep school friends ran to her, eliciting groans and shouts of "no cutting" from those gathered nearby. Reggie growled, ceasing any protests.

His build resembled the bucket people kept dog food in—short and squat with a tight lid that you didn't open at the wrong time. He trimmed his beard and mustache in the "Fu-man-chu-style" of his people and projected a "don't screw with me" aura.

"Thanks for letting us cut, Mr. Dallas." Shaina bounced with excitement. Tegan seconded the gratitude.

*More kids to watch.*

"Just don't make trouble for me in there, and we're good, 'kay?"

They agreed, but he knew better.

When Eryn transferred to the all-girl prep, the two girls were her first enemies. Tegan, a dark-skinned, alpha-bitch, controlled the school through guile and manipulation. Shaina, the freckled redhead, won the puberty lottery and guys hung outside the gates just to see her. Eryn's presence toppled their applecart, and they had gone "mean girls" on her. Eryn wanted to fit in, and peer pressure dragged her into things Reggie had to clean up later.

After the third such event, Landry sat down with his daughter.

*We Perlis don't follow. We lead.*

He taught her how to use their family trait, known as "the stones"—ice-blue eyes that, when applied correctly, caused lesser beings to grovel at Landry's feet.

Eryn learned well.

Shaina fell first, then Tegan. They became minions, doing what Eryn did, liking what she liked. Being a compassionate majesty, though, she treated them like equals, heeding their council or letting them suggest activities. They acted as "besties," but Reggie knew the score.

After what seemed like three lifetimes of listening to crap-rock and teenage giggling, the doors to the venue finally opened. The hall itself was darker than outside; muted light came from smoke-stained wall sconces.

The crowd pushed through security, annoying Reggie, so he pulled the girls to the side and called a security captain over. The hackneyed rent-a-cop sighed, like he knew what the bodyguard already wanted and was prepared to shut him down.

Reggie read his badge.

"Okay, Mr. Melvin, two things you need to be aware of."

"Yes?"

"Number one, I'm a private bodyguard with a license to carry."

That got the man's attention.

"Sorry, but there is a strict no gun policy—"

"The second thing, before you go all regulation on me, is this…" Reggie opened the flap of his suit coat, revealing the stack of money protruding from his inside pocket. Reggie drew out half. "There is enough for you and a few of your most trustworthy men. If things go smoothly tonight, the rest is yours."

The Captain shook Reggie's hand.

"Let me escort you to your seats, sir."

Five seconds after they cleared security though, Reggie shooed Melvin away. Research was the first step to any outing with Eryn. Exit routes were committed to Reggie's memory.

But no plan survives enemy contact and within the ten seconds it took him to excuse Melvin, the girls ditched Reggie. He caught them heading for the general admission floor; a free-for-all space and not in the plan.

"Whoa, ladies. Where do you think you're going?"

Eryn responded as if it was all-so obvious. "The seats you got are too far away from the stage. We want to be right up front, where the action is."

"Those seats allow us quick access to fire escapes should something go wrong."

"Nothing will go wrong," she said. "It's a concert with, like, a million people. I'm safer in the crowd where no one can spot me. Right, girls?"

"I want to be able to reach out and touch him," Star-struck Shaina pleaded.

Tegan provided no help either. "If we're not upfront, we won't be able to catch a guitar pick, or drumstick. We've just got to be up there, Mr. Dallas. Please?"

"Pleeeeease?" they sang in unison.

So much for promises.

Out of his element and over his head, Reggie grunted. He should have brought back-up. Eryn even turned her stones on him, but she had a lot to learn about using them. A person needed total conviction of her place in the hierarchy, which she didn't have yet. Also, the stones never worked on him. He always did what Kynzie wanted anyway.

Reggie knew in his heart that saying no to Eryn was as difficult as saying no to her mother.

Reggie had blown over the part about *two* opening bands before the headliner. The first one reeked of band infighting, and while the second showed some promise, nothing could remove the increasing dread Reggie felt at being off plan. His nerves tingled like live wires. He would have been happier in a room filled with flesh-hungry mummies, but he'd sworn he'd never let *that* happen again.

A compromise put Reggie and the girls holding ground ten rows back from the stage surrounded by rabid fan-bait. In front of them, people pressed against a fence separating the crowd from the stage. Guards patrolled the space in between, watching for mischief and handing out bottles of water to exhausted revelers. Occasionally, they'd pull someone too stoned or dehydrated from the chaos. Security Captain Melvin arrived and pointed Reggie out to his team. There were nods of understanding.

There were advantages to being a deadly-looking dwarf in a pinstriped suit. No matter how close the attendees got, one a look at Reggie, and they backed away. This bubble wasn't big, only five feet around, but it gave him enough freedom to observe.

Packed to the rafters, the majority of female attendees were in their teens to late twenties. Impatiently, they waited on the arrival of their current god of choice. Reggie visualized cartoon hearts in place of eyeballs on upturned faces.

The only potential threat Reggie spotted came in a giant leather-wrapped package. The apish biker dude stood seven feet tall if he was an inch, sleeves bulging with tattooed sledgehammers. The man couldn't make the hole Reggie had, so he just towered over his terminally-embarrassed teenage daughter, while broadcasting her off-limitness. Reggie hoped he wouldn't need to throw down with that beast in a dark alley.

Drawn by his stare, the biker-father took Reggie's measure. They exchanged visual acknowledgments; fellow guardians desperately wishing they were anywhere else.

The lights went down for a third time, and the crowd lost their beehive minds.

"Hello, Music Lovers! This is Dave Long from KLSP! I have the pleasure of presenting to you, *People Magazine's* Sexiest Man in America...

"Nero Wood and Happily... Ever...After!!!"

The curtains parted and colored beams swirled across looming rock monoliths and twisted, reaching trees, setting the tone of the band's fairy tale image. Spotlights traced drums, only to pan away and return, revealing the drummer. The techs repeated this "magical" effect with the bass guitarist, lead guitarist and keyboardist. Their steampunk-esque instruments must have been built by goblins, Reggie thought. They had more knobs and wires sticking out from them than Frankenstein's ass.

Lastly, the lights focused on a painted image on the back drape; an arched stone doorway with writing on it.

The set design recalled the forest portal Reggie and Landry had used to cross into the mortal realm. Bloodied from battle, carrying a baby Eryn wrapped in remnants of her mother's royal gown. No, not recalled—this *was* a painting of *that* doorway. Reggie's nerves went into overdrive like someone danced the Cotton-eyed Joe on his grave.

As *Happily Ever After* launched into their first number, they actually made use of all the gadgets on their instruments. The lead guitar sounded like a Theremin crossed with Eddie's flying V. The drummer played as if he was a one-man tribal circle.

The live music didn't sound like the stuff Eryn had played in the car. It spoke of the marsh outside the Perlis's castle; the ghost-frogs' mournful bleating that calmed and haunted him on summer nights as he walked the parapets. No earthly instrument should have, could have been able to capture that.

And yet, there they were, making him homesick for the realm he, Landry, and Eryn were exiled from.

Who were they? This band Reggie considered a joke until moments before?

Nero, their leader, had still not made his appearance when, on some sort of invisible cue, the crowd counted down.

"3… 2… 1!"

The music stopped dead, and the lights went dark.

A single azure spotlight encased the microphone. Nero Wood materialized through the arch, stepping up to the mic and wordlessly giving the audience a look inside his tormented soul. Black, spiky hair framed a thin, pointed face. Draped in a decayed, white shirt bought at the Max Max store, the rock "god" appeared as if he'd been through a war to get to his fans.

And then there were the leather pants tight enough to make his sperm count low.

Nero's first stanza came without musical accompaniment. He sang it slow and softly as if to a lover.

*"A long time ago, before the world was born,*
*my passion burned for you…*
*My love, the realm of fairy tales,*
*My lust, the stuff of legends…"*

That earned him whoops and cat-whistles. The drummer started a beat that matched Nero's cadence.

*"You've waited since the sun first shone,*
*our kisses only in dreams…*
*And when we finally meet,*
*we'll rip apart the heavens!"*

With an expression of pure rage, he pumped his fist skyward.

As Nero reached the chorus, the band kicked fully into action. Explosives went off, flashes of colored lights burst into life and the crowd transformed into a howling mob, screaming the lyrics with him.

*"When the end of time comes, there will be no parting.*
*When the end of time comes, our story will just be starting."*

Nero Wood didn't just sing… he entertained. He used theatrics to overcome a lack of real talent. Reggie knew the singer's kind, even back in the old world. The song harkened to the inn

Reggie grew up in; a constant trickle of bards desperately hoping for a free bed.

The audience pressed in fast, destroying Reggie's controlled space. The quartet was swept forward until they became part of the lemming-esque crush to the stage. Using what force he could, Reggie pushed back, but there were too many people. The girls and he remained unhurt, but he no longer had control of the reins.

Left with no choice, Reggie eased a string of wooden beads from his pocket. Despite his arms being pinned at his sides, he crushed some of the beads in his palm and scattered the sawdust under the feet of all four of them. Then, uttering the spell that wouldn't be heard over the music, Reggie made a wish.

The elven magic acted subtly. To all but a few, it appeared that the crowd had gotten into a pushing match, those in front versus those from the back. A twenty-foot circle worth of mosh-pitters toppled over themselves. When they righted themselves, they miraculously left a space for Reggie and the girls.

"Ah, that's better."

Eryn shot a displeased look at her bodyguard. Eryn Perlis had to exist in the mortal realm. She wanted to be a normal teenager and normal teenagers didn't have bodyguards who use spells.

Reggie shrugged and gave her a lopsided grin. He wondered if Queen Eryn De Bordeaux, heir to the Fey Realm, would feel the same when the time came for her to reclaim her throne?

Nero, finished with his first set, addressed the crowd.

"Hello! Thank you all for coming out tonight. For out next song, we'd like—" Only Reggie and Eryn saw it, but as Nero scanned the crowd his eyes landed on Eryn for a split second and stumbled. "Um, we'd like to do a piece from our first album."

Tegan and Shaina were oblivious. Eryn, misunderstanding, squealed. "Did you see that, Uncle Reggie? He looked right at me!"

"Yes, and that worries me."

The nagging familiarity of the song, the sets and now Nero himself. Reggie scratched the five o'clock stubble along his jaw in quiet contemplation. Something connected them all. He just couldn't place it. His gut told him he should pull Eryn and the girls out now, but he'd never live it down if he was wrong. He needed proof.

The next song stepped out of character for the band. Loud and annoying hair-band beat with battling guitars that drove the crowd into frantic rhythmic jumps.

Reggie caught motion to the left. A young man came over the raised hands of the screaming audience. "Body surfing," Reggie heard it called.

*Ridiculous.*

Reggie's senses warned him a half-second before another body surfer struck him like a missile. He had no time to brace himself before they tumbled to the floor, the surfer, a girl, atop him. A sting arched up his left arm, and Reggie recognized the pain of being sliced with a blade.

With short, spiky hair and a pierced brow adorned in tribal-looking gear, the attacking surfer was more savage than urban. Large wooden gauges in her ears held lizard totems. Her breath smelled like she'd had rat for lunch.

*Damn! Serpent weavers!*

Reggie kicked the mage up and away, but she didn't land far. As he hopped to his feet, he could see other serpent weavers surfing his direction. Warm liquid dripped down his left sleeve, but he didn't have time to check how badly he'd been cut.

He backed into Eryn, his words urgent. "Time to go."

She couldn't or wouldn't turn away from the performance.

"Time to go, Princess!"

Eryn stiffened at the code word. She turned around as the second serpent weaver arrived. Her reflexes kicked in. Palming her own beads, she crushed them and blew the sawdust forward. The crowd parted, allowing Eryn to drag her friends right up to the stage.

The serpent weavers moved to intercept, spinning and kicking at the bodyguard. Reggie blocked them, making sure their blades didn't strike him a second time. The ladies' bifurcated tongues waved at him in a futile attempt to intimidate.

Reggie launched at them, caught two mages around their necks, and dropped to the ground, choking them to unconsciousness. He popped up into his ready stance as two more mages approached, their blades ready.

Reggie had already drawn his piece. The Boberg XR9-S packed the right punch but wash small enough to keep inside his shoulder holster.

Since none of the concert attendees around them reacted to the fight, Reggie deduced the serpents wove an *oblivious spell* over them. He capped the weavers joyfully without any risk of the crowd turning into a riot. Two quick shots and the weavers' heads popped like bubbles.

Reggie reholstered his piece and moved to join his charges.

Only… they had vanished.

Reggie held Melvin, the security captain by the throat.

"Where are they?"

Melvin gasped the words out. "I…didn't…know."

"What? Didn't know what?"

"That they… were friends of… Mr. Wood's."

Reggie let go of the rent-a-cop's larynx. "Talk."

The captain coughed and rubbed his throat. "My men pulled them from the crowd when your niece said they were in trouble. They were taken backstage immediately. That's when Nero Wood's entourage arrived… saying the girls were special guests of his."

Reggie fumed.

Nero. Everything came back to Nero.

Nero the musician. Nero the performer. Nero who recognized Eryn. Nero who played in fantasy worlds and with young girls' hearts.

When it clicked, Reggie cursed for not having immediately recognized him. Maybe it was the lack of pointed ears. An illusion spell?

Nero.

*Malrion.*

Malrion the Mercenary Bard, last seen a hundred and fifty years ago on the run after kidnapping a regent's daughter. Reggie had been tasked by Queen Kynzie to find the girl and kill the bard, but only managed the first half.

"Where did he take them?"

"They went outside…to his tour bus, I think. We did what…"

Reggie didn't hear the rest, already in motion as he was.

Night swallowed Reggie as soon as he exited the concert hall. Moisture hung in the air from a brief evening rain. His feet found every puddle as he dodged between cars. Scant light poles forced Reggie to heighten his other senses.

Sounds of struggle directed him down an alley to where a tour bus idled. The back window featured a silkscreen of Nero's logo.

Building up speed, Reggie hit full run by the time he leapt, arms over his head, through the back window. He tucked into a roll and bounced off the bed in Nero's private room. *No one.* Reggie pushed through the accordion door into the main cabin.

The girls sat toward the front of the bus at the table. Fear wafted from Tegan and Shaina, but Eryn, dear Eryn, wrestled against the two elven guards holding her wrists.

Even in the poorly lit bus, the elves stood out as *the Elite*—mercenaries for hire. Latte-shaded skin so creamy it boarded on liquid. Copper-colored hair so thick that could have been actual metal. Double-jointed, gaunt bodies that made them nigh-impossible to kill.

The Elite's faces turned toilet bowl white at Reggie's sudden arrival.

*Nigh*-impossible to kill, but not *completely* impossible. Reggie had killed Elite in his escape to Earth, nearly dying with them. He'd do it again for Eryn, if asked to.

Not wanting to waste the surprise, he barreled forward. He ducked low and caught both elves around their waists, letting his momentum carry all three of them forward through the driver's compartment and out the front windshield.

The glass-strewn combatants struggled to their feet.

"Get out of here!" he yelled to the girls. "Eryn, call your dad. Get help!"

Reggie let the Elite draw in close. He took several strikes to his back and kidneys, but only with unarmed hands. He kept the Elite's focus on him, allowing the girls to exit the tour bus.

Squaring off, Reggie kept himself between the Elite and the fleeing trio. Retreating shadows of two girls made it down to the alley's exit, but the last came to stand next to him.

Eryn whispered, "I'm not leaving. Tegan and Shaina can get away if I stay."

"Dammit!" he whispered, but he was all grins.

"What?"

"How dare you think like your mother and put your people first. Now, I'm just going to have to fight twice as hard with you at my back."

Eryn beamed.

Blades gleamed in the alley lights. The Elite pressed Reggie and his teenage charge back hard against the theater's brick wall. Blood dripped down Reggie's arm to the pavement, while Eryn gripped the back of his ruined suit coat. Additional elven mercenaries arrived on scene, but skulked in the shadows.

He'd never reach his beads, nor cast a spell in time, and Eryn had used all hers on the concert floor. The fight would be brutal, but it would be glorious. Reggie stepped forward for his first strike when a nearby door slammed open, the clang of metal against brick echoing through the alley.

Cracking his knuckles, the leather-clad beast of a biker dad from back on the concert floor entered the fray.

"Little miss," he said to Eryn. "Go to my daughter, Darla, right on the other side of that door. She's wearing a wizard's ring that'll knock a moose on its ass." Eryn didn't budge." Go on now, and close the door behind ya. Don't open it again until one of us knocks." He moved to stand beside Reggie. "And stay away from that damn elf, Nero. If I'd known what he was, I never would've brought Darla to this show."

For the second time, the Elite were unable to process what was going on, but then neither could Eryn and Reggie.

"How?" Reggie asked the man.

"Ah, took some bad shit in the Eighties." He scratched his oiled hair looking embarrassed. "Since then, no magic works on me. Especially illusion spells. Saw that tussle with the snake bitches. Figured I'd help."

That seemed plausible enough.

"Do as he says," Reggie told Eryn over his shoulder. "We'll be alright."

One of the Elite moved to intercept Eyrn, but the beastly man caught the elf up by the collar of his black tunic, lifted the elf high above his head, and slammed him down to the pavement. The audible snap of several of the elf's vertebra increased Reggie's respect for the big man.

The biker returned to Reggie's side. By then, the waiting Elite had filed into the alley. They dropped down from scaffolding, rose up from still water, stepped out of shadows.

"The name's Greenleaf. I count sixteen. Eight for you, eight for me?" he asked.

Reggie shook his head. "You already got one. I'll take nine."

Greenleaf raised an eyebrow. "How 'bout we make it a race? Whoever gets to the last pointer wins?"

Reggie's ear-to-ear grin marked acceptance of the deal.

Malrion, a.k.a. Nero Wood, practically skipped. He pushed the gaggle of reporters, backstage fans, and yes-men aside. When he got to the exit door, he flung it open, whirled and exclaimed to all, "Nobody bothers me for one hour. Nobody! Anyone so much as knocks on that bus will be skinned and worn as my costume in Phoenix. Got it?"

The thrill of being in Nero's hemisphere dissolved, and the parasites dissipated.

The plan he'd sold his employers had worked to perfection. Sure, it took years establishing himself on the mortal plane as a rock god, but then he'd had his pick of women while he plotted.

Luckily, girls were the same in every realm. He knew his combination of devilish good looks and heart-pounding lyrics would eventually snare the young queen-in-exile. Nero couldn't to be too obvious or that dog, Reggie Dallas, would catch wind of the operation.

He called to the occupants of the waiting bus as he opened the door. "Oh, Princess? Your king has arrived. I'll have to say, I was shocked when I first saw you. You looked so much like your…"

Nero froze in mid-step.

"Not what you were expecting, eh, Malrion?"

Bruises covered most of Reggie's face, but his wounded arm had been bound. The bodyguard's smile showed off his recently lost teeth.

Nero's head swung left and right, looking for the Elite.

"Dead," Eryn informed him. "Serves them right. They wouldn't have cut it in the army I'm going to build."

The singer slowly stepped backwards, pretending like he'd never arrived.

Instead, he ran into the wall that was Greenleaf. Nero rotated his head up. The biker had a similar patchwork of injuries, but he didn't look as pleased about them as Reggie and Eyrn did.

Greenleaf gave the bard a push, indicating he should re-enter the bus. Once he had, the biker turned his back to guard the door.

Legs gone weak, Nero slumped to a captain's chair. "You can't kill me, y'know? I'm famous."

Reggie laughed, but paid for it with lightning-flash agony.

Eryn, applying gauze to a nasty cut on the back of Reggie's head, reprimanded him. "Sit still, Uncle. If you're going to wear these wounds as badges, I don't want to mess up."

"Famous for what, Mal?" Reggie spat some blood on the floor and another tooth came with it. "The same sappy lyrics you wrote two hundred years ago? 'My love is an oak, a mighty oak.' Geez, why not just say you've got a hard-on and be done with it?"

Eryn slapped his shoulder. "Uncle! Such language around your Queen."

"Queen?" Nero asked.

The teen addressed the man she'd once held on a pedestal. Gone was the crush, the adoration. Eryn showed him only pity. "See? I was okay believing the Fey Realm had nothing to do with me. I just wanted to be a normal girl in love with a pop star." Eryn shaped a heart with her hands and then yanked it apart. "And then you broke my heart when you tried to kill me."

Reggie waved his swollen fingers in a "shame, shame" gesture.

"So, first we're going to ruin your career by having Mr. Greenleaf arrange compromising pictures of you with a goat."

"A lamb," Reggie corrected. "It'll be worse if it's underage."

Eryn slapped his shoulder.

She continued, "After that, I'm going to take my throne back over summer break. If all goes well, I'll have a proxy in place by the time high school starts in the fall."

"Ruin my career?" Malrion whined. "No, anything but that!"

"Be happy it's not your life, Mal," Reggie said, "You're getting off easy."

Eryn finished her work. "Before we start the photo session, you're going to tell me who hired you, and what the situation is back in the fey world. Who's loyal, and who I can't trust. I'm told you know everyone."

"I won't talk." Nero crossed his arms.

Reggie got up and moved toward Nero. "Oh, she doesn't just want you to talk, Nero. She wants you to sing."

And after a few minutes, he did.

# A Bargain Well Met

**Johnny Worthen**

Karmel sat on a wicker chair overlooking the garden but didn't see it. Her eyes were turned inward.

She mourned, not for the last owner of the house—she didn't know her at all—but for her recent string of disaster—which came and came and came and didn't look to end before she was laid beside her Aunt Selwyn.

The roils of fate had brought her here to a fairyland of green leaves and butter blossoms, summer sunlight and perfumed air. Sage, thyme, lavender, and foxglove. She glanced at the verdant scene, but only to take from it the irony.

She'd been there for two hours, straight from the airport, walking the house for an hour, inspecting the rooms and furniture, the keepsakes of a relative she didn't know. When she could think outside of herself, she wondered why her Aunt Selwyn had left her the place. Karmel couldn't recall even meeting her, let alone endearing herself to the point of inheritance.

For the last hour, Karmel had sat still and silent in the back yard feeling sorry for herself.

Behind her, in the house, a bell rang. She acknowledged it but had to drive herself to stand. A quick look in a hand mirror affirmed that her weeping had been on the inside and she could meet the man at the door without embarrassment. She laughed to think that she should still care about such things.

The man at the door, she remembered, was called Lee. She'd contacted him from a bus bench ad on her ride in from the airport. He was nice enough to come that day, time being of the essence.

"Miss Oran?" said the smiling man at the door.

"Yes." She put a smile in her voice.

"I'm Lee Edmunds. I'm so glad you called. We've been trying to list to a property in this neighborhood for a long time."

"Another agency has their hooks in?"

"No," said Lee. "Nobody here sells."

She moved aside and let the realtor in. He surveyed the simple furnishings. "You said you wanted help with the estate as well?"

"Yes," said Karmel. "I need to sell it all quickly and get as much as I can for it."

Lee nodded and picked up a hand thrown piece of pottery with a withered sunflower in it. "Is the rest of the house like this?" he asked.

"Yes."

"Definitely has a style," he said.

"That sounds like a bad thing."

"Yeah…," he said. "There's nothing particularly valuable here. Looks like most of the furnishings are handmade or second-hand twice over."

"I guess my Aunt Selwyn was frugal."

"There's an inheritance tax lien," he said. "Eleven thousand dollars."

"Eleven thousand dollars?"

Lee cleared his throat. "Not a problem" he said. "Since you're not going to live here, you don't have to pay it. It'll come out of the sale price. Don't worry." He smiled and winked, and she tried to smile back.

Of course, there was money owing, another disaster.

But it wasn't. She was borrowing trouble. The sale would cover the taxes. She was making it up, trying to find the bad in the good. Such was her conditioning, and she told herself to get it together. What bothered her though—what she had to ignore was the cruel irony of eleven thousand dollars. That had been the price of her two and half carat diamond wedding ring—the one she'd thrown out the window of her speeding car—deep desert, ten miles out of Albuquerque, divorce papers in a bundle on the seat, Sean's signature already there.

For weeks, she'd regretted her anger. She could have sold that damn ring, started the treatment. Survived, perhaps, to spit in Sean's face and challenge his honor that he was only good "for better" and not "for worse." Coward. Asshole. Betrayer. One doctor visit, three second opinions, a timeline, a price tag, lots of advice to set things in order and Sean was at the lawyer's. "Too much baggage," he told her. "Sorry." She would die alone—he'd seen to that.

Lee said, "But the house is worth a lot, Ms. Oran. I think you'll be pleased. May I see the yard?"

She led him across the living room, musky with rich leather and strawberry potpourri, into the day room, or was it a greenhouse? Do they have they have bistro tables and a settee in greenhouses, she wondered.

The door opened with a creak and they were outside. Karmel heard Lee whistle.

"What is it?" she asked.

"This garden is magnificent," he said.

She looked at it again, wondering if Lee had sensed her trepidation, heard her sadness and disappointment and was doing all he could to cheer her up. She looked again at the green, the yellow, the red, pinks, ambers, whites and violet. She saw then what she had missed before.

There was a large vegetable garden to the right, flowers to the left, spices all around. There was a bubbling fountain where birds splashed. The buzz of hummingbirds joined with that of lingering bees and the air scented with seasonal blossoms and moist earth. Seeing it again, clearly this time, Karmel took in a sudden breath.

"I checked the records. This is a full acre," said Lee, "which is unheard of these days."

"Nobody likes yards anymore," she said.

"It is out of style, but boy, can I use this as a selling point—provided the buyers actually want to live here."

"What does that mean?"

They walked the narrow, cobbled path between the beds, coming upon a rose arbor and grapes climbing a trellis, young birdsong chirping from behind the fleshy leaves.

"It means I'd be surprised if we don't have an offer within an hour from a developer once I put it up. This area is built up. Did you see how big the trees were on the lane? Gentrified area. Better still, since this house was built in 1902, the zoning has changed, and it can be subdivided and have multi-family structures."

"So they'd buy it sight unseen?"

"Around here? Oh yeah. I'd buy it myself if I could afford it."

"What do you think it's worth?" she asked too quickly. She could sense that Lee had heard her desperation.

"Well it depends, but I'd be shocked if we couldn't get a million-two within a month."

For a second time that day, she involuntarily gasped.

Lee smiled. "I get a commission of course."

That might be enough for the treatment, the last chance she could have to see another summer.

She was searching for words when Lee said, "What's all that?"

At the far end of the garden was a wild and unkept place. The beds ended, the path stopped, the human touch removed.

"I guess she didn't get around to—"

"Hallooo," came a voice.

In the fence to the left, a door they had not seen before opened and a woman in a broad straw hat waved to them in gardening gloves.

"I'm Leslie," she said. "You must be Karmel."

"Yes."

"I'm so sorry about Selwyn. She was such a lovely woman."

"I didn't know her at all," said Karmel. "I'll take your word for it."

Leslie's expression shifted, her smile turned confused. "She didn't… Talk to you?"

"No."

"But she left you the house?"

"Yes. Very kind of her. And very timely," she said.

"You are sick." Leslie said as a fact and not a question.

Karmel glanced at Lee and Leslie blushed.

"You were wondering what that area is there?" said Leslie, pointing to the wild place. "I couldn't help but overhear. I was in the carrot bed."

"What is it?" asked Lee.

"It's a Faery Garden," she said.

"Why does the fence end?" asked Lee. Karmel noticed it then too. The fence along the yard ended before the wild area. She thought she could see through the thick tangles of leaves into another yard beyond.

"We all share it," said Leslie. "There are four of us. You can't see it clearly but our four yards touch the area, so it's shared."

"What's a Faery Garden?" asked Karmel.

Leslie fidgeted and glanced at the realtor. She said. "It's an old custom. Brings luck."

"What's with the basket?" asked Lee.

Karmel turned to see what he meant. There was small wicker basket the size of a salad plate, looked to have been made by the same hand who'd make the chair she'd sat on before. She knelt down to inspect it.

"You'll think less of your old aunt if I tell you," said Leslie. "And less of me probably."

There were seeds in the basket and glass marbles. Glittering polished stones. Brown ones—tiger's eyes she recalled. There was a corner of a foil chocolate wrapper, some nuts, some beads, and two half-eaten cookies. Homemade by the looks of them.

"I didn't know her," said Karmel straightening up. "I have no opinion of her at all."

"Excuse me, sir," said Leslie. "You look familiar."

"I'm Lee Edmund, realtor and estate dispensations. You've probably seen me on benches." He handed her a business card and her face went pale.

Karmel tried to guess the woman's age. Though she talked and acted like a thirty-year-old, her hands betrayed her when she took off her gloves to take the card. She was old. Seventies at least.

Her eyes were bright and wrinkled. Her hair was once chestnut but was now frosted in gray.

"You... you're going to sell the place?" Leslie asked.

"I need the money."

"Because you're sick," she said. "You have what Selwyn had."

"I doubt it," she laughed and knew it sounded bitter.

Lee cleared his throat again. "I'll get all the paperwork together tonight and meet you tomorrow," he said. "We can have the listing up right away. You won't have to wait long."

"That'll be fine," said Karmel.

"Then I'll leave you two," he said. "I'll see you tomorrow, Miss Oran.

"Don't forget about the furniture and stuff."

"I won't."

He disappeared behind a row of corn, beans climbing their stalks, squash at their base.

"Selwyn lived to a hundred and four," said Leslie. "She made ends meet at the Farmer's Market."

"May we all be so lucky," she said.

"The basket is for offerings to the faery folk," said the neighbor. "We all have such a thing. Mine is a china plate. My grandmother's. Aaron uses a copper cup. Linda, a river rock she found."

"That's quaint," she said. "I should probably—"

"It brings luck," said Leslie. "The offerings. Also, no one goes into their garden. We all have gates like this one. You may come over any time."

"That's very nice, but—"

"A hundred and four," she said her eyes staring hard at her. "Living here. With your disease."

"That's not true," she said. "It's fatal."

"Everything is, but you'll be surprised what a good diet and good relations can do for one."

She was feeling tired. The doctors had told her to take it easy. They had suggested hospice, a place that could care for her as her mind decayed in anticipation of her body. In six months, she wouldn't recognize herself in a mirror. In ten months, there'd be nothing to look at.

Unless the treatment worked. It hadn't yet, not on anyone, but there was a chance.

"Selywn had no daughters," said Leslie. "She was the niece of an aunt who also had what you have. She lived to ninety-nine."

"Sure."

"Your sister has a daughter?"

"She's unmarried. I don't like her."

"She'll have a daughter. You'll see."

"I won't be here."

"Karmel—"

"Leslie, I'm very tired. It was nice meeting you. I'm sure whoever lives here next will be equally as nice."

The neighbor nodded her head once and disappeared behind the fence. Karmel took a step into the wild brush and then thought better of it. She took a dime from her pocket and dropped it in the basket before going back into the house.

Lee had left note a on the counter. *We'll need to get a surveyor here immediately to make claim to that shared area before it becomes an issue. I'll arrange for it and fencing. See you tomorrow.*

She fetched the vodka from her suitcase and drank straight from the bottle. She rested on the settee and drank more, trying not to think of Sean, of her bitch sister, of the disease that had a name so long and obscure and obscene that she hadn't bothered to learn it.

She dozed in and out, waking to nightmares of divorce papers sent to her with the medical bills. She saw overdue notices, her car repossessed, her friends not answering when she called. "She was a downer," they said, when they did not know she could hear them. In the twilight between sleep and waking, in the stupor of the alcohol and pain pills, she heard the doctors apologizing to her as if they were to blame. How she wished they were. She could strike at them then for the loss of her life. Twenty-four-years-old, maybe twenty-five, when her friends might see her again to plant her in the ground.

Ground and soil. Worms and roots. Flowers and stems. Gossamer petals of marigold and daisy. Dandelion, wonderful and edible, medicinal, but called a weed. So strange. So strange.

In the last light she remembered where she was and thought the house was simple and beautiful and hoped the next inhabitants would deserve it as she did not. She was wrecked and already dead.

"Selwyn's niece," came the voice. "Be ye drinking without sharing with us? Did your aunt naught teach you manners?"

She pulled herself to sitting and poured a drought of drink into an open acorn held by a blue… a blue winged—

"It's beginning," she said. "The hallucinations."

"Well if you're too far gone to pour, I'll be mother to the others."

"Help yourself," she said and laid back. Her head swam in booze and whatever the hell the pill was. They told her the pain could come as a migraine, crippling and long. The narcotics were for that, to keep her screaming down, but she'd been using them for cocktails for a month now and the doctors knew it and gave her all she wanted.

They had it wrong though. The hallucinations came before the migraines, not after.

She watched as the little blue man fluttered his wings and wrestled the bottle into the air. Then with the help of a white and orange fairy, he poured drops of her liquor into little ceramic cups, the size of thimbles. They were like the homemade vase in the hall with the wilted flower.

"Here's to Selwyn's niece!" said the blue one.

And they raised their cups.

She counted six, all with dragon-fly wings, no two the same color or pattern. Half were men in loin clothes, the women were in knee high summer skirts, floral and breezy. Barefoot all, flowers in their hair.

"Call me Karmel."

"You rude lout!" cried one of the women, a pink rose colored one with subtle yellow stripes, tiger-like in the moonlight. "You want to talk manners! You're pouring her liquor and we haven't been introduced."

The blue man floated up into the air and Karmel could feel the breeze. The best hallucinations touch all the senses. He was the color of a cornflower, and his wings beat out the smell of lilac that chilled her skin around her neck to gooseflesh.

"You're right Sparkly," he said. "Thanks for keeping me honest."

"Get on with it."

"Kind Karmel, I am Dewwalker. That is Sparklyrose. She has a sharp tongue but soft lips I do love to kiss."

"Dewey!" Sparklyrose said and blushed. When a rose faery blushes, their cheeks turn crimson. How strange, how strange, thought Karmel.

"That there is Mudsy. Mudspatterday, if you need to know it all." A tan and brown spotted male nodded and raised his cup. It looked too heavy for him to hold, as the bottle seemed impossible for them all. She raised her glass in return.

"Bitterbulb," said Dewwalker. "She's the young one. Barely eight score and three."

Karmel took the bottle and poured more into her glass. "A score is twenty so… what? A hundred sixty-three?"

"Aye, a real brat."

"Shut up!" said the small one.

But they were all small. Bitterbulb stood maybe three and half inches tall as were all the females. The males were four, four and a quarter inch at most.

"Can I measure you some time?"

"No!" spat Bitterbulb.

"Don't mind her," Dewey said. "She's a brat."

She stuck her tongue out.

"Then we have Longvine and Grasseed," said Dewwalker. "That's it for the welcoming committee."

"Happy to meet you all," she said and drained her glass. She could not taste the alcohol at all. Not a good sign. She'd be wrecked in the morning.

But who cared?

"Drinking alone isn't good," said Sparklyrose. "Lucky for you we were nearby."

"Lucky."

"Do you have any whisky?" asked Mudsey.

"Or beer?" said another.

"Just vodka. Prescription strength."

"It'll do," said Dewey.

She shrugged.

"So, will you be changing the house much?"

"I won't live here," she said. "I'm selling it. Probably to a developer. This week."

"What?"

"No!"

"You won't be a caretaker?" asked Sparkly.

Karmel shrugged and shook her head. The movement hinted at the hangover to come. Pain was in her future. So had it been for a long time now.

"Why?"

"I'm sick."

"Posh."

"Posh? What is that even…" There were now twelve faeries as her eyes saw double. She coughed and felt suddenly and direly nauseated. "I don't feel good," she said and tried to stand.

"You can't be selling the land," said Sparkly. "What would become of the garden."

"Condos."

"No! Why would you do such a thing?"

"I'm dying," she said.

"And?"

"And I'm dying fast."

"That can be helped."

"Maybe. Right. That's maybe." She tried to put her feet beneath her, swiveled and aimed but kicked the air like an upturned tortoise. "I need the money."

"There, see?" said Mudsey. "It's always money with these. The garden will go. Not a wild place in all the city left then. We should tell cousin Beetle to expect us directly."

"There's the other three."

"How long can they last with *condos*." The word was spat as an epithet and it made Karmel giggle.

"I don't want to leave the city," said Bitterbulb sullenly.

"Oh hush," said Longvine.

"Darling," said Sparkly, "darling can you hear me, Miss Karmel? Do you really value money that much? Can you not be happy with a simple but bounteous life?"

"It's not the money really. It's that the money is for the doctor who said… that maybe… there's a chance. You know? Invasive therapy in Annapolis. It might…" She fell back onto the settee and the room spun at speed.

"Darling, Selwyn had the same. We can handle that old thing—"

She caught the first throb in her throat, and it stopped the spinning for a while. She shifted and found the floor. She dropped her head into her hands and spoke to her shoes.

"I couldn't stay here if I wanted to. There's eleven—"

She caught the next one in her mouth, but just barely.

Sensing the inevitable. She stood up and staggered outside. She fell to her knees over a pile of clippings earthy and warm and threw up until she passed out.

She dreamed of fairies and long conversations, of taxes and deserts, loneliness and purpose, of the love of a dead woman who lived in this house for eighty years before giving it to her.

She awoke covered in dew. There was a smell of sick, but her mouth was not foul.

She had no headache. No hangover. She wasn't even thirsty. She couldn't remember a time when she'd felt better than she did this day.

Standing, she shook her head to test it. Flowers fell from hair. The first light crept over the house and touched her ear. It was warm and caressing.

The house was open and quiet. The garden was open and still.

She followed the path down toward the wild place, piecing together her dream trying to recall the moment that this feeling began—this calmness and beauty, obligation and love.

She was not afraid then, she was not sad. She was curious.

At the edge of the wild place, she knelt before the basket and pushed her fingers into the rocks and seeds and shiny things.

She felt it with her thumb and pinched it with her fingers.

She lifted it to the light and the diamond in the ring dazzled her as it never had before.

# Friends of the Kakamora

J.D. Mankowski

The Dead Man's Chest opens at sunset.

No neon lights, velvet carpets, or roped lines draw attention to it. The bar's entrance exists in a vacant alleyway between Kinzie and Grand. A rusty tin sign hangs above the door, but the bar's name isn't written in words, but shows only the engraved icons of three skulls and an 'X'.

The dozens of pubs, restaurants, and cafes that surround the alleyway keep The Dead Man's Chest from getting too much attention. The patrons who have found it say it was by happenstance, and all of them note that it was the sweet aroma of tropical fruits that had first caught their attention. The nondescript door, the ominous tin sign, the lack of windows or insight on the establishment creates a sense of intrigue to all who find it.

But not all can enter when the bar is open for business.

For a limited time, a bamboo handle appears on the cast iron door. It isn't by magic, but rather a series of well-crafted cogs and springs. The door itself, one might say, is a gateway with the humor of a cuckoo clock. Its detail is impressive and uncommon for a bar so close to downtown. Many people have found the door and its handle, but few have successfully pulled it open. Those denied entry argue that the door handle scans for fingerprints and only people on a private guest list are actually allowed in. But those who enter steadfastly maintain the facade that the door opens simply by luck.

And luck is only the first key to getting inside.

Once through the door, the Dead Man's Chest greets its potential patrons by shepherding them through a dark and narrow hallway. The sound of waves, the taste of sea salt, and the faint chirping of island birds and insects occupy the rather empty antechamber. Guests walk through the dark in single-file for seconds, minutes, sometimes even hours, and not all of them ever make it to the bar. In the hallway there are two possible endings: the first being another cast iron door with a bamboo handle appears. This door is the exit, and without the option of turning back for a drink, the Dead Man's Chest will usher the guest back out into the alleyway.

Turning left is the second key.

If luck should have it while walking through the dark, instead of the exit, guests then find a descending staircase illuminated in dark blue light. A towering wall of human skulls looms over the stairs as guests are beckoned into further darkness. Some joke that the skulls belong to every patron who's come before them, others say the establishment used to be a Halloween shop. Glowing paint is brushed along the collection of skulls to spell a phrase in childish scrawl: *Friends of the Kakamora.* Like the exit door, once a guest comes to the top of the stairs, there's no way of turning back. An overwhelming sense of curiosity pulls them forward.

The sounds of ocean waves, birds, and insects stop in an instant as the descent towards the Dead Man's Chest truly begins. The narrow walls gradually break free of standard form. The staircase opens up on either side into an alien-like aquatic cove with bioluminescent fungus, pools of glowing blue water, and stardust gathered on stalagmites. It's an impossible feat, but the artistry of scale, with a touch of smoke and mirrors, gives the impression that the cavern stretches for miles in either direction. But just as quickly as the silent cave appears, it then vanishes when the staircase becomes wrapped up in brickwork and darkness again.

The long walk ends in a vestibule of sand filled with other lucky guests.

A thunderous roar rumbles from above as a waterfall crashes against a glass-domed ceiling. Only a few steps across the sand awaits the final door. It's a large arched piece of driftwood, adorned in golden seashells and barnacles. This is the door that leads into the Dead Man's Chest.

A sign reads: "Please Remove Your Shoes for the Kakamora"

Only a few in the crowd smile knowingly as this is their first or second time returning. They take off their shoes and tuck them into bamboo cubbies mounted on either side of the door. Others whisper disconcertingly to each other, because not everyone from their party made it into the room. They glance back at the staircase, waiting for them to appear, but chances are that their friends or family are back outside, in the alley, and will not be allowed in tonight. Eventually the guests give up waiting, and all the shoes in the room are removed and placed in bamboo boxes along with cell phones, jackets, and watches.

Then the driftwood door shudders and splits down the middle. Another masterpiece of cogs and springs operate silently into action. The two pieces of the door swing outwards, inviting the crowd inside.

Now they can enter.

Now they can drink.

The Dead Man's Chest is a perfect beachfront paradise at night.

Once honored guests pass through the door, they find themselves on a narrow sand path between two large dunes. Their view of what's ahead is obscured by a slow bending curve. The door behind them dissolves into the fallen ruins of an island temple. Stones and toppled statues litter the pathway and dune beds above. The Kakamora's great city is partially lost to nature's own magnificent jungle that grows out of the darkness. The crashing waves of the ocean call guests forward. The warm, humid air is inviting.

The scale and size of the Dead Man's Chest is unimaginable.

The starlit sky above appears distant, but the full white moon feels close. Its light bathes the pink tinted sand and highlights the softly glowing blue and purple shells. At the end of the dunes, guests arrive at a lagoon. Tin drums and a gently strummed bass guitar play from hidden speakers.

Centered under the moon is an ocean, its waves are as real as the ocean spray it sends onto the shore. A long bamboo bar with twenty stools is also situated under the moon. A transparent wall filled with bottles of elixirs, messages, and ships stands behind the bar. A single bartender smiles in greeting; their arms inked in the ancient tales of the Kakamora.

A group of guests sit at the bar. It is their first time in the Dead Man's Chest, and they are overwhelmed by the experience. They gravitate towards what they understand; towards what they expected. Guests are given menus that have been tucked into worn leather tomes. They have come for drinks, but the menus themselves are derived from the history of the Kakamora. To order anything is to request a tale of the inhabitants.

The Bartender is swift in movement, but graceful in tone.

Guests watch as their drinks are made right before their eyes; a dazzling spectacle of acrobatic tosses and turns. Bottles are pulled from the shelf and replaced twice as fast. There is no time to write down the contents or measurements of the drinks. Elixirs, spice blends, chunks of fresh fruit, and if watched closely, a scroll or ship might be added depending on the order.

For guests seeking seclusion, the Dead Man's Chest suggests a quieter space.

To the far right of the bar, tucked behind low foliage and scattered torchlight, there are private palm leaf-thatched bungalows for two. Luminous glass jellyfish chandeliers slowly twist in the island breeze. Glass tentacles chime and ring quietly. Plush feather seats are split by tea tables made of coarse island wood. Guests are invited to sit on the ground and listen to the natural sounds enjoyed by the Kakamora until the servers come.

Unlike the Bartender, the servers will not tell stories, show off their tattoos, or amaze guests with a spectacle of circus mixology acts. These servers will come and go as silently as the Kakamora, dressed in dark floral bandeaus and skirts. The servers don't provide menus. They simply read the guests and return with what they know to be the best beverage for sharing.

The drinks come in many different styled basins intended for two. The Conch Shell is a guest favorite with its fruit punch and spice-blended flavor with sugar-crystal straws. It bubbles and froths cold mist as it floats to them from the bar.

This is only the beginning.

It doesn't matter where guests stand or sit, a view of the sand-centered stage between the dunes and the bar will always be available for the many acts displayed by the talent in the Dead Man's Chest. All performances involve fire.

Two twin fire baton twirlers are the first to arrive. They're agile tumblers with playful expressions. They make the crowd laugh as they pretend to be envious of the other's favor and applause. Their whirling flames change from sea green to a cheerful yellow, but their act ends when a flame juggling high-trampoline jumper appears.

From out of the dunes half-a-dozen more arrive. Some, guests recognize, are the silent servers from the bungalow. The performance starts with a literal bang, and the jumpers fly up into the air. The sand that all guests first crossed to the bar is now found to be rubbery and flexible. Clouds of pink dust ripple outwards as the jumpers and jugglers bounce, flip, and toss flaming clubs. They shout to the audience, and the audience echoes the words back. It's gibberish but feels right upon their tongues. Some of the spectators become so enamored with the show that they join the jumpers. All are invited to soar up towards the sky, and this alone brings more laughter throughout the room. Then flaming clubs flash like bright flares. It forces the onlookers to blink, and by the time they've wiped spots from their eyes, the jumpers are gone, and the ground is solid once more.

Finally, a master of the flaming whip arrives. Guests are shown back to their seats. The Master and the bartender are hard to distinguish. Some who have been served glance back at the bar to see if the Master and Bartender are one and the same, but this is not so. The Master tells the history of the Kakamora, and his flaming whip swirls, spirals, and bends into shapes that complement the tale. There is the occasional 'crack' that commands the audience's attention. The Master says fire is humankind's gift to the Kakamora, and that it would be dangerous to let the Kakamora dwell in the dark. The stage and room fall silent. The whip sizzles and hisses in the sand for a moment. The audience finally remembers to breathe as the moonlight dims itself behind a set of wispy clouds.

The night is coming to an end.

A symphonic spectacle of fireworks and rockets battle against the sky. Without clocks or phones to judge the time, it is only by this event that anyone knows their time at the Dead Man's Chest has finally come to a close. The moon will always triumph despite the guests' wishful thoughts. It descends into the ocean and pulls with it the ocean tide. Servers usher first time visitors out through the dunes. Each are given a token if they promise to return. Guests collect their belongings and climb the stairs. There is no hallway at the top, only a black cast iron door with a bamboo handle. It opens into the alleyway between Kinzie and Grand. The first rays of daylight fall upon the city streets beyond.

The token is a brass compass that always points back towards the door with the bamboo handle.

After visiting the bar for the first time, guests are eager to get back. The token, however, is not a free pass through the first door. The brass compass is nondescript, as if purposefully ordinary. It does not capture the experience of the Dead Man's Chest the way many guests wish it would. The inside of the compass has an ordinary face with black lettering to mark the cardinal directions. The inside of the compass's cover has the icon of two skulls with the words, '*Friend of the Kakamora*'.

Should a guest be lucky in the days, weeks, months, or years to come, the arrowhead of their compass eventually turns blue. The token does not behave this way for all guests, nor does it happen for all the members of a group at once. Those who are impatient wait the longest.

The door in the alleyway lets any first-time-returning guest with a blue arrowhead enter. Those who stand in the alleyway after being rejected by the door say that the compass is the key, but all compass holders know that the real key is luck, and nothing more.

The same dark hallway welcomes returning guests and new guests alike, but the blue compass arrow guides those who've been invited back to the stairs and antechamber below safely. These guests wait the longest under the thunderous waterfall, but the disbelief of returning has them abuzz with excitement. They share stories in hushed voices about their first time at the Dead Man's Chest. Some haven't been back in decades, a few guests have only waited a day or two, but the details of the Bartender's tales, the jumpers and tumblers, the ocean breeze, and perfect drinks brings them together—all are instantaneous friends, and friends of the Kakamora.

The rest of the guests file in. Those who have lost friends and family in the hallway above are slow to surrender their shoes, cell phones, and watches. Then the door made of driftwood shudders and splits down the middle. It slowly peels outward and invites the guests in.

Now the returners are welcome.

Now they can drink.

The compass hums gently in the palms of first-time-returners.

As a first-time-returning guest walks through the valley of dunes, their compass begins to vibrate. The blue arrowhead glows and points to the left side of the bar. The token offers to guide these guests away from the lagoon, the Bartender, and bungalows; though the choice ultimately remains with each guest. Some stay and follow newcomers to the bar, eager to learn more about their friends, the Kakamora. A few couples race towards the bungalows, having missed the intimate space during their first visit.

The rest of the first-time-returning guests move together in a pack towards the ocean waves that crash loudly against the shore to the left of the bar. Through shadows cast by the jungle trees, a bed of towering dark sea rock breaks free above the ocean tide. Moonlight illuminates a small series of steps cut out of the stone to give guests safe passage up. Their compasses spin clockwise endlessly. This is where the Kakamora want them to be.

Circular booths, lined in silver, with tables made of coral, are embedded in the crown of sea rock.

The guests intermingle and seat themselves. The view from their castle-like structure looks out onto the sand stage below. The back of the lagoon bar twinkles and glitters through the glass bottles filled with elixirs and ships. The sweeter smells of the lagoon are lost to the fresh ocean breeze. The air is refreshing to the point of invigorating. Once again, the guests are chattering excitedly amongst themselves.

As they sit around the three large coral tables, it takes time before any of them realizes there are carvings in the table's surface. The ocean spray that fills the grooves slowly catches the moonlight, until the various rune-like carvings glow in a similar shade of blue as the compass arrowheads.

The centers of all three tables dissolve to reveal deep luminous pools of bubbling water.

Through the center of the tables, Mermaids swim up with bright and welcoming smiles. Their skin is pearly white with gemstone scales adorning their arms and torso. Their eyes are turquoise like the water they swim in, and their voices carry a calming melody. The guests are astounded. It is hard to separate the costume from the person swimming before them. The mermaids, used to the surprise, showcase their fins, gills, and webbed hands. They seat themselves on the inner edge of their pool. None of the guests are quite sure what to believe but are enraptured by the mermaids. Lists of drinks shine suddenly, displayed in puddles of water on the tables.

No individual drinks are served here.

Each group must decide on one drink to share. They are all friends of the Kakamora, and every drink can be the right choice according to the mermaids. The menu displayed in the reflecting pools show a large conch shell beverage akin to the one served at the lagoon below. Another is made in a vibrant waterlily, and the final drink offered is served in an old sunken treasure chest. As each table makes their choice, that particular drink vanishes from each menu. The first group of guests choose the conch shell, as many of them have already enjoyed it in the bungalows below. The second group selects the treasure chest based on its mystical appearance. The final table is left with the waterlily, but they agree that they would have been satisfied by any of the three.

The mermaids dive back into their pools of water, giving the guests one final wave with their iridescent fins. It is the last time they will see their servers. Minutes later, large sugar glass bubbles float up from the water below. Contained inside are the drink orders for each table; a larger-than-life red waterlily, a silver conch shell, and a treasure chest detailed like the driftwood door.

The first-time-returners drink merrily as the fire performance starts. The baton twirlers arrive and pay attention to only those in the lagoon. Then the tumblers and jumpers come with their flaming clubs, and all the returning guests agree that the sea rock provides a much better view. Then the highest jumper plucks a star out of the sky and throws it out to them. White fairy dust explodes above the crowd. The guests cheer and wave and the jumpers free of flaming clubs smile and wave back.

Finally, the Master returns with his fiery whip and tale of the Kakamora. Again, he warns them that the Kakamora love fire, and it must be gifted to them by friends. Despite their distance from the stage, the guests hear the Master's voice clearly even while competing with the ocean waves. As their drinks are emptied, the guests turn in their seats to catch a view of the moon. The fireworks begin.

To visit the Dead Man's Chest a third time, a guest must have partaken in drinking from the treasure chest.

In the days, weeks, months, or years to come, guests that drank from the chest receive a golden coin in the mail with a handwritten invitation. One side of the coin has an engraved icon of three human skulls. On the other side, the words 'Friends of the Kakamora' is written. The invitation is made of thick paper, and it smells gently of vanilla and sand warmed under a tropical sun. The ink itself is written in fluid cursive that transitions between black, blue, and green without pause, like ocean ripples.

*Dear Guest,* the letter reads, *You are cordially invited to join us at the Dead Man's Chest, we thank you for your continued patronage, and eagerly await your arrival. Please bring this token as proof of invitation and wait by the driftwood door to be escorted to our exclusive Bamboo Room. No date has been specified, please arrive at your own time.*

*Sincerely,*
*The Kakamora*

By now, the guests know the way to the Dead Man's Chest and seldom do they wait longer than a day or two to arrive. A third-time-arriving guest waits beneath the rusted tin sign before sunset or shows up after many eager patrons have been rejected by the door. It is easy to spot a first-time-returning guest because they flaunt their blue arrowed compass. Gold coin carriers, however, are more protective of their token. They are the real friends of the Kakamora, and do not seek the envy of others. More so, to protect the exclusivity of the Bamboo Room, third-time-arriving guests keep their coin pocketed and away from prying eyes.

When the driftwood door opens and the evening begins, only a few guests hang back as the rest of the crowd moves towards the lagoon. Now, the final guests reveal themselves. Three or four, if any at all. Together they talk about the Bamboo Room and are pleased to know that none of them actually know anything about it. They imagine the grandeur and honor of being invited to this special room. None of them know what they've done to deserve it.

A little person appears in the archway of the driftwood door.

It is gender ambiguous and silent. The guests don't always notice their chauffeur as quickly as they should, but the little person waits patiently because it is friends with the guests. It, with its little potbelly, furry feet, and wide green eyes is a Kakamora. When the guests notice the little person, they recognize it to be their friend as well. After all the stories told by the Bartender, the Mermaids, and the Master, it is uncannily clear to them who this little person is.

The Kakamora doesn't speak.

With a welcoming smile the Kakamora removes its coconut hat and bows to the guests. The guests are compelled to bow back in kindness. Then the Kakamora wiggles its hips in excitement. The grass sewn skirt it wears makes a rustling sound. This causes the guest to smile, for they know that this is how the Kakamora communicate. Finally, the little person opens one of its small hands and waits for each guest to give back their golden coin. Some guests feel slighted, as they've grown fond of the coin and its secret prestige, but they know it will be worth it once they've been taken to the Bamboo Room.

The Kakamora makes the gold coins vanish before motioning for the guests to follow.

Instead of going through the dunes like everyone else, the third-time-returning guests make a 'U' turn with the Kakamora and walk into the ancient runes of the forgotten city. The guests are intrigued by the excursion and whisper to one another. None of them knew how far back this side of the Dead Man's Chest went. The jungle trees and broken pillars block most of the moonlight. Between the shadows, guests can see clay bowls, broken wicker baskets, and polished bones. The soft swishing of Kakamora skirts multiplies the further the group goes. Other little coconut-capped heads pop out of the stonework and bushes. They, too, smile and bow before trailing behind the guests with gleeful giggling. The walk would feel more unnerving if it wasn't for the basins of firelight illuminating the other end of the ruins.

A bamboo door painted in gold shimmers up ahead.

Old stones and thick tree trunks form a wall between the guests and the Bamboo Room. A small treasure chest identical to the one they have all once sipped from sits on a little stage by the door. The Kakamora that has led the guests here leaps onto the stage and smiles. The parade of other Kakamora begin to cheer in high-pitched, laughable, joy. The Kakamora opens the chest to reveal hundreds of other gold coins before adding a few more. The golden door slowly opens with a heavy weighted groan. Blinding white light pours over the guests. The Kakamora chant a single word again and again. 'Friend, friend, friend…'

The guests are confused, but one of them eventually steps through the door and their choice is met with cheers. Another guest might follow, but more so out of discomfort and fear. The Kakamora continue to cheer. If a final guest or two remains, it's because they no longer want to join the other patrons in the Bamboo Room. This disappoints the Kakamora, but they only show it with very sharp toothy grins.

Now the Kakamora have humans to give them fire.

Now the Kakamora can feast.

# Between Two Worlds

**Kevin Nielsen**

Aerto surveyed the shimmering portal before him and wondered if this was the time he was going to die. Visiting his mother was, after all, the most dangerous thing he did each year. Still, in one hundred and eighty-seven years, he'd made it back out alive every time, just not always having successfully reached his mother. The silver-white hair of advanced years bore testament to that, even with his Fey blood.

A figure manifested before him. Stifling reflex, Aerto stopped himself from drawing his athlas, a three-branched throwing knife enchanted to always return to his hand when cast. The mortals would call this glowing, sculpted image of perfection before him an angel, sent from an otherworldly, omnipotent deity above. Aerto knew it for what it really was, simply a creature of the Fey, though attuned to a specific Path—a watchman, guardian, and guide at the entrance to the spirit realm.

"Three choices stand before you," the figure began, then looked up and, upon seeing Aerto, grinned. "Aerto! Your mother said you'd be calling today. Didn't expect you for another hour at least."

"Only have twenty-four hours to get there and back again. May as well make use of all of it."

"Such a short time. Perhaps you should consider—"

"No," Aerto cut him off.

"But your mother—"

"No."

"True immortality—"

"No!" Aerto clenched and unclenched his fists, resisting the urge to punch the achingly handsome face before him. "What are my options today, Fey? How shall I start?"

"You're no fun," the Fey man said, then waved a hand. Three colored symbols appeared in the air before him.

Aerto reached out and touched the symbol of crackling lightning without hesitation. The three symbols pulsed for a moment, then all vanished. In his hand, Aerto's athlas began to tingle with energy.

"A wise choice," the Fey Guardian said, smiling with perfect teeth set in a perfect mouth. "I wish you luck on your journey, cousin."

Aerto's hand was moving before the anger registered, athlas spinning from his grip just as the Fey faded from the mortal plane. The athlas spun out for twenty yards or so before reversing of its own accord and returning to Aerto's hand.

Cousin? Just because Aerto was half Fey, something he would never admit to anyone not already one of the Folk themselves, did not make him that creature's cousin. What blood they did share had caused over a century of sideways glances, muttered curses, being shunned, physical and emotional abuse, and the eternal damning judgement from the true mortals among whom Aerto lived. Few truly knew what he was, but something inside them, something primal, recognized and feared him. And fear inevitably led to pain, as Aerto knew all too well. He suppressed a shudder and checked his belongings one last time.

Satisfied his equipment was all in place and he was as ready as he'd ever be, Aerto took a deep breath, made ready his athlas, and stepped into the portal. His mother was waiting in there. Somewhere.

In the moment between fully materializing and non-existence, Aerto breathed, which was impossible, but still, he did it anyway. In that breath, he took in the room into which he would momentarily enter, a large rectangular space with short, half-walls dividing it into an annoying sort of maze. Fey bats, massive things larger than a medium-sized dog, swirled about within the room, and what looked to be several spiders skittered down one wall, each the size of a small mortal child.

Aerto materialized and, in the same instant, his athlas flew from his fingers, expertly bouncing off one wall and then taking a bat full in the chest. Immediately crackling lines of energy leapt from the bat and shot outward at all the other monsters in the room, slightly wounding each. The impaled bat hissed out a cry that turned into an abrupt, gurgling choke as Aerto's second athlas, thrown less than a second after the first, sliced the bat in two. Like the first athlas that was also charged with lightning from the 'angel's' magic, this athlas shot out streaks of lightning, striking the surrounding monsters. The two athlas spun through the air, moments apart, curving back toward Aerto's waiting hand. Aerto grinned and flipped his hood up onto his head, blocking out distraction. In his mind, he calculated his next move, and then the next, and the next. In a blur of motion, Aerto snatched an athlas out of the air even as he dodged a stream of red acid shot by one of the spiders. Spinning, he sent the athlas back out, cutting down another bat and wounding all the others with the succeeding lightning blasts. Still spinning, Aerto's other hand grabbed the second athlas as it arrived and threw it in another direction entirely, killing a monster and bouncing back against another, killing both, before spinning back toward Aerto's hand. In mere moments Aerto was alone in the room as the last monster corpse slowly puffed away, like smoke in the wind. In the opposite wall from where he entered, a new portal bloomed into existence.

Aerto grinned in grim satisfaction. Less than a minute from his first breath in this room to the appearance of the next door. He remembered a time when it would have taken him five times as long. At this rate, he would make it through the first five rooms and meet the first 'angelic messenger' faster than ever before. The odds that it would be his mother were slim, but, well, despite himself Aerto still had hope that this time, this one time, the trip would be a simpler one. Determination rooted his grin into his clenched jaw and Aerto stepped through the portal.

The second room fell almost as quickly as the first. The only difference was the addition of several monster-plant hybrids that spat balls of sticky acid. Dodging them added a second element to the melee that simply heightened the skills Aerto had to deploy. Still, less than a minute later, Aerto stepped through the next door and into the third room. That room added a strange water element to it in the form of a long trench filled-to-bursting with ice-cold liquid, but the monsters again proved little challenge. This time, before the portal opened, three new glowing symbols appeared in the air before him. His hand trembled in anticipation and the thrill of battle as he reached out and touched one of the symbols, eager to use this new ability in the next room.

He wished some of the things that worked here, in these passages between realms, would be replicated in the mortal realm, though the magic of the Fey worked differently. It would be nice to have these same sort of defenses and protections while out in the mortal world and defending its inhabitants from the monsters and other horrors that escaped the pockets of the world still controlled by ancient Fey magic. His athlas worked, but to empower it with electricity, or flame, or poison, or even with double shot, were beyond his abilities. Here, however, such enhancements were so commonplace as to only be noteworthy in comparison to the mortal realm. Shrugging to clear his mind, Aerto stepped through the portal and into the fourth room.

His athlas flew from his hand a split second after materializing. It flew toward the closest monster, a ghost-like ghoul that lobbed balls of explosive fire, and struck with the devastating fury of a lightning bolt. As before, blots of energy shot out at all the other monsters in the room, striking and wounding each. This time, however, the athlas also bounced off the initial monster and ricocheted toward the closest monster. It struck, simultaneously sending out blasts of energy and then continued on toward the next beast. Aerto hurled his second athlas, expertly throwing it so it curved in the air and struck a monster hiding behind a half-wall partway across the room. The first athlas returned to his hands a second later and Aerto dodged to the side as a ball of acid shot past him. Turning, he threw the athlas, but before it reached its target, the second athlas took the monster in the throat. The creature, another giant spider, faded from existence as both weapons returned to Aerto, who stowed them away. The next room would be a rest room, an 'angel' room. He wouldn't need his weapons. Not physical ones, at least.

Aerto hesitated before the portal after it appeared. His hands shook, so he stuffed them into the pockets of his cloak and tried to ignore them. He licked his lips, took a deep breath, and stepped into the portal.

Another humanoid Fey Guardian appeared in the room before him. For half a moment, as he recognized the creature as a female and he thought he'd finally gotten lucky. That moment passed almost before it began when the woman smiled at him, showing perfect teeth, a flawless face, and violet, almond-shaped eyes. It was feminine perfection, stirring every inch of his decidedly male body, but it was not his mother.

"Aerto," the Guardian said, her voice a breathless, haunting call to beauty and longing. "Your mother is eager to see you. She speaks so highly of you."

Aerto grunted. His tongue seemed fixed to the roof of his mouth. He hated dealing with Fey women. Mortal women were simple. They fell for the alien, Fey aspects within him as easily as a fly into a spider's web. He'd had his pick of them all, which had, at times, landed him in trouble with any number of lawmen and husbands. Fey woman were predators and ensnared him with even greater ease. Thankfully, his Fey blood allowed him to keep some wits about him.

"Such a pretty face, Aerto," the Fey continued, eyeing him with hungry eyes. "It's a pity you haven't taken your mother's offer to become one of us. We could have such…fun."

"No, thank you." Aerto said, finding his voice. "I'm just here to visit my mother. What boon do you offer in this quest?"

The Fey woman's ruby-red lips turned down into a frown and Aerto's heart broke a little. It was readily apparent why the mortals considered these women, the Guardians, to be angels, messengers from a benevolent diety. They were that, messengers, at least, but benevolent they were not.

"You're no fun at all. Why bother even visiting if you're not going to stay eventually? You'll age, you know, out there in the mortal world. Here, in the Between, you'll be a true Immortal. You'll be perfect, a pillar of—"

"What boon?"

The Fey woman growled, and the sound was like shattering glass. Aerto refused to wince, though the sound tore at his insides.

"Healing or increased speed," she hissed.

"Speed."

The Fey woman waved a hand and Aerto felt a warmth spread through his body. He'd done this enough in his one-hundred and eighty-seven years of life that he instantly recognized the enhancement magic. This was at least partially replicable in the mortal realm through the means of various potions or spells, though limited in duration. The Fey magic here, however, would last as long as he remained within the Between. The warmth passed quickly, but Aerto was moving toward the portal on the opposite side of the room before the spell had taken full effect.

"One thing, Aerto," the Fey said, making him look back over his shoulder at her. "Your mother asked me to offer you this one reminder. There will come a time when you need her and she will not be able to be there. If you wish to escape the realm of death, there is but one choice left before you."

Aerto stepped through the portal.

Twenty rooms and four more angels later, Aerto felt weariness creeping into his movements. He'd only been in the Between for a little over an hour, but he'd already almost passed through half of the passage. In the last few rooms, he'd taken a few hits and missed a few of his throws, despite the added skills he'd gained along the way from each of the angels or the various rooms that provided a boon once he'd killed all the monsters within. In the mortal realm, he'd be a hero of stunning renown, untouchable to all but the most powerful and feared even by them. Here, it was proving barely adequate to keep him moving forward.

And, to be honest, his mind was distracted, travelling elsewhere through the realms of memory and emotion. Each angel had born messages from his mother, warning him of troubles to come, imploring him to remain and become a true Guardian, begging him to be one of them. Aerto was ashamed to admit part of him desperately wanted to accept that offer. To be immortal, to have the powers that these creatures had. Invincibility, or the nearest real equivalent, was an intoxicating possibility. Yet, he remembered those he protected back in the mortal realm, all the children and townsfolk he'd saved over the last century. They needed him, even if they didn't know it or judged him poorly for his Fey heritage. They were babes next to him, needing protection, education, and shelter. No, he couldn't abandon them— not for something that would only benefit him, not even for his mother. Sighing, he stepped through the portal and into the next angel room.

A demon held his mother by the throat in the center of the room.

Aerto immediately readied his athlas to throw, ignoring the burning flames that leapt from the demon's skin and roasted the air around it. The demon turned its red, pupil-less eyes toward him and opened a maw full of pointed, jagged teeth.

"Fool," the demon hissed. "Would-be hero, here to gain glory. Watch me destroy this creature you would worship. Watch and feel as your mind breaks beneath the strain of crushed belief."

The hand around Aerto's mother's throat tightened and lifted her into the air, her feet dangling. Despite the flaming hand around her neck, Aerto's mother turned her deep-blue eyes toward her son, the light in them undiminished by her predicament. They beseeched him, imploring him to run and save himself.

Aerto straightened, athlas spinning in his hand, a blur of flame, lightning, steel, and poison. He crouched and drew his second athlas with his off hand, face twisting into a snarl. He would not abandon his mother. The demon clearly had no idea who Aerto was. If he had, perhaps the demon wouldn't have tried it, but such was not the case. Aerto growled, and something primal roared up within him, surging through his veins. This was his mother. The woman who stood behind his yearly sojourn through the Between, a place within which no mortal trod. The woman who raised him for over forty years, who gave him his athlas and trained him how to fight, to live, to believe.

No demon would have her.

Aerto threw both weapons at once, aiming low at the demon's massive body. The weapons flew true, but before they hit their target something struck Aerto on the back of the head and he knew no more.

Aerto awoke some time later, head throbbing and eyes heavy. He mumbled something and tried to stand but couldn't find the strength. How long had he been unconscious? Where was he? A cool hand touched his face and Aerto recognized the soothing touch of his mother.

"Hush, my son," she said, her voice velvet, smooth and soft. "All is well."

"Are you well, Mother?" Aerto's voice was a croak, but he forced it out anyway. "The demon…"

"Was never much of a threat. He was simply there to get—well, we'll have plenty of time to talk about that later."

Cool dread washed through him. "What do you mean?" Aerto forced his eyes open, meeting his mother's pale, blue, alien gaze. She stared back at him, expression intent, earnest, and unyielding.

"We'll have plenty of time to talk. You're one of us now. A Guardian."

"What have you done, Mother?" Aerto struggled to stand up, to even sit up, but his body simply didn't have the strength and just lifting his head made his vision swim. What had she done? "How long have I been out?"

"Two days."

Aerto sucked in a breath then let it out in a hiss. That was it. He was done for. He could never leave the Between now. His time among mortal men was over.

"Why? I've told you… you promised… I…" Aerto's voice faded away in to ragged, angry coughs.

His mother smiled down at him and, for the first time, Aerto noticed the sadness hidden in the corner of her eyes.

"What was the first thing I taught you as a child? Do you remember?"

"Never trust a Fey."

"I'm sorry, my son, but also, I am not. This is as it must be. I love you."

Aerto swallowed and ground his teeth together, ignoring the pain throbbing in his head. He leaned his head back, though kept his eyes open, fixed on the one creature he loved most in the world and found he hated her as well.

"Never trust a Fey," he whispered, and wept.

# His Glass Prison

Martin L. Shoemaker

I tried to calm my breath as the shop door closed behind me, a little glass chime sounding as it did. *Inconspicuous, Laura, inconspicuous.* I couldn't get caught. Couldn't get trapped.

This place had to have a back door. I didn't know these stores and I had just slipped into the first door at random. I had never been to this plaza before Rodrigo had dragged me along as a lookout for his job.

Rodrigo. Bastard. Thinking about him, I couldn't stop seeing that grin on his face as he fled while I had struggled with the rent-a-cop. *He* lifted the jewels, and yet they made *me*, and I got nabbed. I knew what he would say: *Mala suerte, puta!* Rodrigo had no friends, just people he used. I knew that. But somehow, I had thought it was different with me.

A knee to the balls had freed me from the detective. I had ducked down lanes in the plaza at random, trying to lose him. Finally I had come in here, through a small door between two windows full of junk. Looking around, my first guess was an antique shop. Small porcelain statues, brass bowls, wicker dolls, and tiny framed pictures were everywhere, arrayed on small tables covered with lace doilies or old shawls. Thick, colorful rugs were strewn across the tile floor. A table in the rear was covered with a large, golden silk shawl decorated with a circle, a triangle with three smaller circles, and some foreign letters. I didn't recognize the style, but it might be worth lifting. Beneath the shawl something bulged, something maybe the size of a volleyball.

Behind the table, the wall was done in an elaborate mural, some woodland scene of a couple on horseback.

The air was thick with piney smell. Two shelving units were full of candles in varying sizes and colors, and three of them were burning. Dominating them was a blue candle, almost as long as my forearm, set in its own triangular brass stand.

No prices on anything. It all looked like junk to me. But just in case, I kept an eye out for something small worth stealing. The silk shawl might sell to a collector, maybe. Whatever was under it was probably valuable, but way too large to hide.

Suddenly the mural parted, and I realized that it wasn't a wall, but an elaborate beaded curtain. A woman stepped through, short and dark-haired in a colorful silk blouse and black silk skirt. She wore a floral bandana rolled into a band on her forehead, holding back her bangs. She was maybe late twenties or early thirties, but not really old.

"Ah," she said in a musical hint of an accent, "a beautiful lady visits, just as I have foreseen. You come to have your fortune told?"

What a come on. "A beautiful lady." Yeah, right. I never dressed up on a job. The point was to be inconspicuous, so you dress down. But even when I made an effort, the most I might pass for was "cute". Never beautiful. Not like this con artist with the fortune teller scam, *she* was beautiful.

I knew the scam. You don't live on the streets as long as I have without learning a lot of cons and schemes. I had even worked a few when things got tight, before I had fallen in with Rodrigo. So, I knew better than to fall for her line.

But again, I wanted to stay out of the plaza for a while longer. So, I decided to play along.

"Yes, I… would like to hear my fortune. But I… don't have any money."

She wouldn't believe that, but she expected to work on me to get the price up. She would offer me just a tease, use it to entice me to pay more and more as the drama mounted. I wanted to settle on the lowest number possible, though I hoped in the end to skip out without paying at all.

She wasn't deterred. "Money is not the issue here. *Fate* is the issue. I feel it gather around you. You've come to Princess Lyuba just in time. The wrong move tonight could be your ruin. The right move… your wildest dreams." Oh, she was good! "Sit. We must prepare you for your great destiny."

Lyuba pulled two chairs from the wall and placed them by the table. Normally I hate to be played. I can't stand being controlled, confined. But I was only pretending to be hooked. I was in charge here, I was free, so I could play her game.

When she removed the gold silk from the table, I saw what the game was: the old crystal ball gag. Cold reading, with the crystal ball to distract the mark. I had seen cold reading a few times, and it could be persuasive. I would watch this woman's technique, maybe learn something.

The ball was very good crystal. It magnified everything with flawless clarity. It sat on an ornate gold base. That and the ball were the only things I had seen that were worth stealing. I didn't plan to grab anything with her watching, but I liked to plan ahead.

I sat in the chair closest to the door—just in case I needed to make a break—while Lyuba stood on the other side. I looked her over, trying not to be obvious. "Princess Lyuba." My ass. She was dark enough she could pass for a gypsy for the act, especially with that accent. She probably practiced it in off hours. But I would bet money she was a Latina playing a gypsy for the con.

Lyuba carefully folded the shawl into a small triangle. Then she pulled the candle and its stand up next to the table. I never saw the match; but I smelled sulfur, and a flame rose from her fingers and lit the candle. However she had palmed that match, she was *good*.

Then she sat and began her spiel. "By the Three Powers, the future shall be revealed."

The flame wavered, and I noticed how cleverly she had placed the candle. The flickering light shone through the crystal ball, drawing my eye. I made myself ignore it. Never look where the grifter wants you to look.

Lyuba leaned over the ball, her thick black hair flopping over the floral bandana and hiding her eyes. Her voice lowered, both in volume and in pitch. "I see… someone is looking for you."

Interesting hook there: non-specific, and yet mysterious and grabbing. Of course, a store detective *was* looking for me. That gave me a bit of a shiver. That's the trick of cold reading: say something that can be interpreted in a hundred different ways, and then let the mark choose the interpretation. When you see what he falls for, give him more of it.

"I see it is… a man. He comes from a long way away." Oops! She blew it there, too specific. *Hey, "Princess", maybe I should be running this con!* I knew she was fishing for a reaction she could build on, but I was careful not to give her one.

But then she got *very* specific, and I wondered what her game was. "He is very far, yet right next door. The glass… keeps him from you." What could that mean?

Then something in the corner of my eye struck me as odd: the candle flame was very steady, but the light in the crystal ball was moving. How did she do that? Maybe the light wasn't from the candle at all? Maybe she had some other light source as part of the gimmick. I stopped listening to Lyuba's routine. Despite wanting to look cool and uninterested, I couldn't stop myself from staring at the light.

And then it started to grow! No longer just a white dot, there were colors, hints of detail. Parts of it were… moving. I stared closer, and I saw a very tiny figure walking, arms and legs swinging. And it was walking towards me.

What was this? Some sort of hologram shit? How could a small-time con artist in a shabby little shop like this afford that?

Soon I made out more details of the figure. Definitely a man—part of Lyuba's con, no doubt—the man who was looking for me. Heh. I should be so lucky. He was *hot!* Tall, dark wavy hair… And muscular! He looked like he could snap Rodrigo in two. He wore some sort of Robin Hood style outfit, lots of leather. The green silk shirt barely contained his chest. His wavy hair fluttered in some wind passing through the crystal…

No. I was falling into her trap. The wind was part of the hologram, not in the crystal ball.

His eyes… As he got closer, I could see their color, a silvery blue. They were looking right at me. I swear, the hologram locked eyes with me! I couldn't stop myself looking back. His face was as strong as the rest of him. This was a powerful man, but something about him looked… helpless. That's the only way I could describe it: those eyes were pleading, as if he needed something from me. As if, if I just leaned closer, he could tell me what it was. I couldn't help myself, I leaned closer.

Somewhere far away, I knew, the gypsy was still giving her patter. I wasn't listening. I strained to hear what this man had to say. For now I could see that he *was* talking, shouting even, but I couldn't hear him through the glass.

*Stop it! He's not in the glass!* But the illusion was so convincing.

And then he actually reached out and put his hand upon the inner surface of the crystal ball, as if he was trying to reach out to me. As if I could somehow pull him out of there. Without thinking, I reached out and put my hand to his.

Lyuba batted my hand away. "No! Do not touch the crystal!" While I had been enrapt in the hologram, she had snuffed the candle. Now she swept the silk cover over the globe.

Shaking myself back to reality, I sat back in my chair and nodded in appreciation. "Pretty good trick, lady, how'd you do it?"

Lyuba glared at me. "What is this nonsense you speak?"

I pointed at the lump under the silk. "The guy in the glass. How's it work? It's a hologram, right?"

"You… You saw him?" Suddenly Lyuba's eyes turned fiery.

"Oh, come on. You wanted me to see him. What's your game?"

"You! You're a thief!"

She was closer to the mark than I cared for, so I tried to deny it. "I'm no thief, lady."

"You are, you're a thief! Trying to steal the Three Powers." Lyuba stood and grabbed a broom. Even angry, she stuck to the gypsy clichés, waving the broom around like a club. "Get out of my shop! Go!"

Knocking my chair over, I ducked the broom and headed for the door, dodging around all the junk in the way. Lyuba chased after me. "You will never have the Three Powers! Thief! Thief!"

She chased me right out of the door—and right into the arms of two police detectives.

The cops hauled me into an interview room for questioning, but they had nothing on me.

I *could* rat out Rodrigo if I wanted to. He had no idea that I had trailed him one night, following him back to the whitebread suburb where he was just Rod Garrett, everyday family man—with a workshop in the back full of merchandise from jobs he had pulled in the poor part of the city. *My* part of the city. I never planned to use this knowledge against him, but I didn't like anyone having control over me, so I made sure I had a hold over him if I ever needed it.

Karen Lewis, the female detective, played good cop. "Work with me, Price. I can help you here, but you have to help me first."

The bad cop, Mike something, leaned his old wooden chair back against the wall. "You're wasting your time, Lewis. Ms. Price is too stupid for her own good. She's gonna take the rap for some hustler who couldn't give a shit about her."

Nice try. He had the act perfect: razor stubble, messed-up hair, the faded gray suit with the sweat-stained white shirt—a tired detective who would just as soon lock me up as talk to me. But this wasn't my first interview, and I wasn't intimidated.

Karen leaned her butt against the table where I sat. She was a contrast with Mike: properly neat in a well-tailored blue skirt suit. She tried to lay on the sympathy, fake warmth in her voice. "Look, Price, we don't really want you, but you're all we've got. We'll take what we can get, but we really want your boss."

Inside I seethed. *Rodrigo's not my boss. I have no boss! No one owns me.* But I wouldn't let her goad me into a reaction. I wouldn't let *her* control me, either. I would wait them out. Eventually they would have to admit they had nothing, and I'd be out. If I was *really* lucky, I wouldn't even have to ask for a public defender and deal with all of that.

Oh, if I gave them what I knew, Rodrigo was heading for hard time, five to ten for sure! But I would keep quiet. Then I'd hook back up with Rodrigo, and he would owe me big time. Either he would give me my split and a bonus for taking his heat, or… Well, I knew the combination for the lock on that workshop.

But Karen was persistent, I'll give her that. "Come on, Laura. Can I call you Laura? You don't want to deal with the court. We don't want to deal with the court… unless it's for someone who's worth our effort. So what do you say? We don't even need something to put him away. Give us just a name, and we can do the rest, and we'll get you out of here. Give us a name and a location, and I might be able to lose any record that you were ever here."

I kept quiet. Mike leaned forward, the front legs of his chair slamming into the floor tiles. He stared at me, his eyes full of anger. "You can't do that! Don't give her anything."

"She's small time, Mike. We can do better. That's right, isn't it, Laura? You're small time. Give us someone big time, and you're gone." They had this act down pat.

But I wasn't falling for it. I might not be Princess Lyuba, but I'm pretty good at reading people. They were out of cards to play. I was almost home free. I just stared up at Karen with my best wide-eyed innocent look and said, "I still don't understand what you think happened here. I was minding my own business, and that perv started chasing me. You should arrest him for stalking young women. He probably watches them in the dressing room. When he chased me, of course I ran away and hid."

Mike stood up and paced across the room, then turned back to me. "So you're sticking with that story, huh? That's all you have to say?"

Even though he had nothing, Mike wasn't ready to give up. So finally, I played my trump card. "Well, that and… I think I need a lawyer." It was their move now, put up or shut up. They weren't going to take this up a notch, I was sure of that.

Mike called my bluff. "All right, that's the way you wanna play it." He pressed the intercom button on the wall. "They still backed up in booking?"

"Yeah, Mike," a woman's voice. "There's at least an hour wait, might be as many as three."

"Fine." Mike looked at his watch. "We don't have time to deal with this." He pushed the button again. "All right, send someone to take Ms. Price down to Holding. Book her whenever they get around to it. No rush once she's out of our hair."

Wait. No. They were supposed to blink when I asked for a lawyer, not make me sit… in a cell…

The door buzzed, and Karen gently but firmly tugged on my arm and pulled me to my feet and towards the door. As I resisted, her push became more insistent. Mike knocked on the door. "Comin' out!"

The door opened and a uniformed policewoman on the other side took my arm and led me into the hallway. The dingy yellow linoleum floors and the stale smell in the air only added to my sudden anxiety. She walked me towards Holding. I could almost feel *it* approaching. The lights grew dimmer as we neared the end of the hall – or maybe it was my eyes.

*No, they can't do this. They can't actually mean it.* We got to the big faded wooden doors with "HOLDING" painted across them and the officer pushed me through.

The air in Holding stank of sweat, puke, piss, and not nearly enough disinfectant. The room was crowded with uniforms and perps on every chair or bench. It was a big boxy area with bars breaking it into a number of small men's and women's cells, each large enough for maybe three or four prisoners. I hated it on sight. My skin crawled, my heart raced, and I fought to keep my breathing steady.

The officer pulled me over to a sergeant at a desk near the cells. "I've got one for ya, sarge, until they clear up holding. Where do ya want her?"

The sergeant rose and pulled a key on a chain from his belt. "Cell number three has room. She'll be nice and cozy in there." Cell number three had two women in it, hookers judging by their clothes. One leaned against the wall, glaring out at the sergeant. The other sat on a low bench, curled into the corner, a glazed look in her eyes. She was tripping on something, for sure.

I could see the key. I could see the lock. The sergeant reached to open the cage…

I turned and gave them everything on Rodrigo. I could *not* be locked away.

*Mala suerte, Rodrigo!* I didn't feel too bad about what I'd done. He ditched me when things got hot, now I had ditched him. I wouldn't wish five to ten on anyone, but the bastard had always treated me like he owned me. I'd always known I would have to fix that someday. Thanks to the cops, it turned out this was someday.

Oh, I might miss him a bit. We had some good times, and he was great in bed. But I couldn't let myself get tied to him. He never really meant anything to me. He wasn't anybody special. He wasn't like… the guy in the crystal ball.

*Stupid, stupid, stupid Laura! Falling for a con like some… some mark!* But yelling at myself still didn't get that guy out of my head.

The trick was so real! If I just figured out how Lyuba did it, break her hold on me. Then I could put her and the crystal ball and the mysterious man behind me.

At least, that's what I told myself as I broke into Lyuba's shop.

Breaking and entering wasn't my specialty. Short cons, lookouts, lifts, smash and grabs… Those were my usual style, low risk work without much chance of getting caught. But what I had done many times for Rodrigo was case a place that another team would then hit. I'm pretty good at going unnoticed, just a nobody in the crowd.

It only took me a couple of days to look the shop over, figure out Lyuba's routine, and find my way in. She had no alarm system, just that damn bell over the front door. That was no problem. I wasn't planning to go in through the door.

There was an air vent in the rear of the building. The cover was bolted down, but the bolts might've been put in before I was born, judging by the rust stains running down the wall. A little work with a hacksaw and I had the cover off.

The air vent let into a little room. This was the only weak spot in my preparation: without going back into the shop and risking Lyuba recognizing me, I couldn't be sure what was behind the bead mural at the rear of the shop. It turned out to be part storeroom and part office. The vent was over a small desk, which I dropped carefully down onto. The tiny bit of alley light that snuck through the vent showed the desktop was very neat, unlike Lyuba's shop, so I didn't have to worry about knocking anything over. I set the vent cover back, hooked and taped it in place, and the room darkened almost completely.

I crouched in silence on the desk, letting my eyes adjust. There, I could see the floor and just enough to find my way to the beads. I lightly pulled them aside and I peeked through the bead curtain.

This was the riskiest part of the whole job. Lyuba had pulled the metal grillwork across the windows before locking up for the night, but light still shone through from the plaza outside. And that meant light could shine out, too, so I couldn't risk any of my own. I had to rely solely on the streetlights. Again, I waited for my eyes to adjust until finally I could make out shapes in the room. It didn't look like anything had changed.

And there it was: the table with the silk shawl and the large round shape hidden beneath. Gently I moved toward the table, keeping one eye out for movement in the windows. I reached for the silk.

As my fingers drew close, a bright blue spark arced from the shawl with a loud *pop!* I was momentarily blinded and my fingers tingled. I knew silk could give a static zap, but I had never felt one so strong—or seen one quite that shade of blue.

I froze, fearing someone outside might have seen the spark. But there was probably no one out there this late at night. And besides, the spark was probably not as bright as I imagined. It just seemed bright with my eyes adjusted to the darkness.

I grabbed the shawl—no spark—and I slipped it into the canvas bag I had brought. I wasn't here for the shawl—just the crystal ball—but it was silk, and pretty fancy, so it might be worth something. Some of this other stuff might be valuable to a good fence as well…

Then I remembered: the only good fence I knew was Rodrigo, and he had been arraigned that morning. The police had found quite a haul in the workshop, and the judge had denied bail. He said Rodrigo was a flight risk—which he was. So, no sense in loading myself up with heavy stuff I wouldn't be able to fence. But the shawl was light, and it was already in my bag.

I looked at the crystal ball. Amid a faint glow from within the glass, there he was, waiting. Watching me.

*Stop it, Laura!* It was getting harder to convince myself this was a trick. It looked *exactly* like he had been there patiently waiting for my arrival. His head practically filled the sphere. His eyes watched me, tracking me. I couldn't see where the light came from, it just was there in the crystal.

Then the man stepped back, deeper into the crystal, until I could see him from the waist up. He reached out and put a hand to the surface as he had before. I put mine to the glass.

Again there was a spark. The glass was warm, almost as if there was actually a hand just beneath it.

*How did she do this? How?* But I couldn't spare a thought to figure that out. I was too distracted by this man. The look in his eyes, pleading… He needed something from me. He needed… me. And I needed him.

*No!* No, what I needed was that crystal ball. If I took it someplace, studied it, figured out the trick, *that* would release its hold on me. At least that's what I told myself, but one way or another, the crystal ball and the man inside it were leaving with me.

I reached to pick up the ball and put it in my bag, but as if he could tell what I was up to, the man shook his head. *Are you trying to confuse me?* He wanted to escape, I was sure of that, but he was stopping me.

*Speak to me. Tell me what you need.* Nonsense. I was trying to communicate with an illusion. But despite myself, I was sure he was trying to communicate as well. He was shaking his head and holding up three fingers. Lyuba had spoken of Three Powers. Despite myself, I held up three fingers as well.

The man nodded. Then he held his hands out in front of him and moved them slowly, hands together, way out in front of him, then far apart and closer, and then back together right up against that muscular chest. He repeated the gesture, as if he were tracing out a square.

A square? It was like somehow, we were getting on the same wavelength. I *knew* what he wanted. I reached into my bag and pulled out the shawl. He nodded eagerly, and I put the silk back into my bag.

Then he held up two fingers; and suddenly I laughed out loud. I looked out the window to make sure no one was out there, but I hadn't been able to help myself. It had suddenly struck me: here I was in the dark, two in the morning, breaking into a gypsy's shop, stealing stuff… and playing charades with a hologram.

The man didn't understand what was so funny. He just kept pointing over toward the wall. When I was sure no one was coming, I felt my way over to the wall and carefully waved my hands until I felt… wax. *Of course.* I picked up the big blue candle and brought it back to the table, and the man nodded again. Into the bag went the candle.

The man held up three fingers once again, and then he spun around, arms outstretched. I knew what he meant, honestly, but I was enjoying the view too much to stop the show.

When he finally stopped spinning, I grabbed the crystal ball in both hands. Smiling, he ran all the way forward, put his face right up to the glass, and kissed my palms. Again, I felt a shock, though I was sure I was imagining it.

Into the bag went the crystal ball. I grabbed the base it sat on as well, just in case the hologram projector was in there. But despite how I tried to rationalize, I knew the projector couldn't be in there: the man remained visible and active even after the ball was free of the base. He smiled at me. I would do *anything* for that smile.

Even Mrs. Whitebread Garrett didn't know about Rodrigo's cabin in the mountains. This was his most secret hideout; but one night in bed he had made the mistake of mentioning it to me. After that I managed to go through his trash once and find an electric bill for Rodney Geers at an address way upstate. One Trailways trip and some hitchhiking later, and I had confirmed where the place was: far out from a little hick town, at the edge of electrical service, in the middle of nowhere. Rodrigo had stashed guns and some cash and food here in case he needed to hide for a long stretch.

Now I had returned. Rodrigo's old lady wouldn't disturb me, and Rodrigo would be gone for a good long time. I would have time and privacy to figure out the crystal ball. I built a fire to warm the place up, and I lit a cigarette to calm my nerves. Then I sat on the cabin floor and set the crystal ball on its base. The man was there still, patiently waiting; and we resumed the charade-talk.

After a pack of cigarettes and nearly a day of waving hands and mouthing words back and forth, I couldn't help believing—the guy in the crystal ball was *real*. Not only that, he really was *in* the crystal ball. It wasn't a scene from somewhere else, he was actually trapped there. I don't know how he breathed, what he ate, or where he went when he walked away and shrunk down to just a point, but he had waved and gestured and pounded on the glass until I knew he couldn't escape.

I didn't want to believe it, it was nonsense, but I believed all the same. And my heart broke for him, trapped in that little space for who knew how long? The idea horrified me. For a long time, I couldn't bring myself to look at him. Just thinking about how that… that gypsy bitch had trapped him like that made me sick to my stomach.

I wanted to get him out. I wasn't sure how, but there had to be a way.

I held out my hand to the glass again, and he caressed mine through the surface. When we did this, I almost felt like he could read my mind. I thought about rescuing him, and he nodded and smiled. This was what he wanted. This was the reason our paths had crossed. But how?

I got up and went through Rodrigo's cupboards, looking for, what, I wasn't sure. But then I saw a hammer. Maybe? I brought it back to the middle of the floor and raised it to smash the crystal.

The man shook his head furiously. Then he raised his arms as if to ward off a blow. The fear on his face was unmistakable. Breaking the glass might kill him.

But then what to do? I sat and stared at the fire, and I wondered.

When I looked back at the crystal ball, the man was knocking on the glass, as if I could hear him and he could get my attention that way. Once I finally noticed him, he traced the broad square with his hands. *The shawl.* I pulled it from my bag, and he nodded. The shawl was key to his rescue, I was sure. But what to do with it?

I spread the shawl out on the floor next to the crystal ball and looked at it. It didn't look like anything off the rack. That big triangle and circle design, the strange letters… It looked handmade, unique.

Then I noticed that the man was holding his hands up, fingertips and thumbs touching to make another triangle. I looked from him to the shawl and back again. It was the same shape. This was important somehow.

*Three Powers…*

Each point of the triangle ended with a large circle. I suddenly realized that the circles were the perfect size for the base of the crystal ball. I stood and picked up the ball and the base, and the man nodded, but when I set the base on one of the circles, he shook his head. I set it on the second circle, and he shook his head again.

When I set it on the circle closest to the fire, he nodded, so I set the crystal ball down on the base.

Three circles. Three Powers. This was crazy, I knew that, but I was going to try it, crazy or not. For the second circle, the answer was obvious. He knew what he was doing when he had made me bring the blue candle. I pulled it from my bag and held it over the circle farthest from the cabin door. He shook his head, so I held it over the circle nearest to the door. He nodded, and I set the candle down.

But what was the third circle for? He hadn't pointed out anything else from the shop. What went there?

I looked to him for an answer, and he was waving both hands down in a clear gesture: *Sit, sit.* So, I sat on the third circle, my butt barely fitting with my legs crossed in the triangle. *Now what?*

The man looked at me, disappointed. I was letting him down. He expected me to have this all figured out by now, but how? This was all crazy, all outside of my experience. I was treating this like it was some kind of… some kind of magic shit, like I expected another blue spark to appear and free him from the glass prison. Was I losing my mind?

Well, maybe I was. But one way or another, I had to know. There was a candle. Candles are meant to burn. I pulled out my cigarette lighter, lit it, and set it to the wick.

Instantly the candle poured fourth smoke, a strange blue smoke the same color as the candle itself. It started as a thin stream, but it grew thicker. Soon it was billows, then it was clouds. Then it filled the room. Between my sudden coughing and the smoke, I couldn't see the fire… or the crystal ball… or the man…

Eventually the smoke thinned and finally cleared away. The man stood in the circle, arms spread wide, shouting up at the ceiling in triumph. But his shout was still silent, and his image was… distorted, like it had been in the glass, but different. And he towered over me like a giant. The whole room was distorted as well. My eyes must be watering from the smoke. But I didn't care, I just rushed forward, eager to feel those massive arms embrace me—

—and I smashed my face and body straight into some nearly invisible wall. "Ow!" My cry fell oddly flat, deadened. I felt around in front of me, and found a smooth, curved surface. I could get very close to it, but I couldn't get through.

The man looked toward the cabin door, so I did too. The door was open, and Lyuba walked in. Like the man, she towered over me. She ran up to him, and he threw his arms around her. *Bitch!* That was supposed to be *my* embrace!

They kissed for a long time. Finally, they looked down at me and laughed. And then they left the cabin… left me in my small glass prison.

I pounded on the glass until I thought my hands were broken. I shouted until I was hoarse. Then I leaned on the glass and cried, slowly sliding down the sphere until I lay curled in the bottom, sobbing.

They had used me. They had gotten me to do exactly what they needed. They needed someone they could trick into switching places with him, someone greedy and needy – and someone who thought she was too smart to be conned. They needed a thief.

That's what I needed: Rodrigo! Either I could get him to find a mark, or I would trick the bastard into swapping with me himself! Rodrigo would get me out of here one way or another!

In… five to ten…

# Final

Michaelbrent Collings

Reminder: your final exams have begun. Projects must be turned in under the solstice moon, at the ring of trees in the center of The Wood.

—

FROM: RG@feyschool.edu

TO: O@feyschool.edu

Esteemed Lord and Greatest of all Professors,

I hope this missive finds you well, and I appreciate your willingness to make yourself available outside of normal hours. I also thank you for your choice of final exam—none of the other teachers are offering a practical test as the final, and I am really looking forward to it.

Alas, that is also where I'm running into a bit of trouble. I think the instructions are very clear as to the *purpose* of the exam. But I'm a bit unsure whether you are looking at urban, suburban, or agrarian environments; and to what extent the test subjects are available for our use.

I don't think anyone else is reaching out to you this way, so I hope this isn't construable as cheating, but I thought it worth the risk.

Your humblest of students and most servile of servants,

RG

—

FROM: O@feyschool.edu

TO: RG@feyschool.edu

RG,

First of all, you are correct: your question is definitely construable as cheating.

So, kudos.

The instructions state "anything goes." That includes seeking advantages over the other prospective graduates. Only a few are chosen each year, and the rest… Well, given the stakes, I'd *hope* you would cheat whenever and wherever possible.

So, does that mean it is no longer cheating, given that I have provided tacit approval? No idea. Nor do I care. You may proceed as you see fit. Decide for yourself on the environment, and how far to go with the test subjects. This is not a kindergarten class (and yes, I know that "kindergartens" haven't really been invented yet, but such is the nature of My Sight). Figure it out for yourself.

- O.

—

FROM: RG@feyschool.edu

TO: O@feyschool.edu

Great King O.,

Thank you for the information in your previous letter.

I have decided to work in an agrarian environment. A lot of the others are doing so because they think it will limit damage and/or exposure to your Sight if/when they make errors. Not exactly bold thinking on their part, and I've included an attachment with the names of those fifteen students so engaged (for information only; of course, I have *no wish* to see them punished, or any hope that they fail the test).

And, lest you think I have similar motives—I *am* choosing a less-populated area, but it is simply because of the isolation such a location will allow. In other words, I don't want to limit the rest of the world's exposure to the experiment, I just want the subject to truly experience what is happening, and to experience it *utterly alone.*

And, side note, I *like* the way blood spatters against trees.

Your student and servant,

RG

P.S. Thank you for allowing the use of computers. I know we won't always have access to things out-of-stream like this. But they are fun. I enjoy playing Fortnite, and the pornography available is almost—*almost*—corrupt to the point of Fey.

Attachment: *prospectiveclassmates.culled.docx*

—

DORM POSTING:

FROM: O

TO: ALL STUDENTS

RE: Test/Extra Credit

Two reminders:

1) You should have your subjects chosen by now.

2) Extra credit is now available! Those who wish to avail themselves of it may answer the following (to be turned in at the same time as your final exam projects):

**How should those students who fail this test be destroyed?**

Extra points for creativity, quality of pain, and duration that the killing can be made to last.

A few of you may notice that this means any who attempt the extra credit but do poorly on the test will also run the risk of suffering the fates they themselves have devised. This is intentional.

—

FROM: O@feyschool.edu

TO: RG@feyschool.edu

RG,

My assistants inform Me you have been refusing to provide updates on your progress. Please check in. This is part of the grade.

- O.

—

FROM: RG@feyschool.edu

TO: O@feyschool.edu

King O.,

My subject has been chosen. A farmer. He lives alone, and I am just trying to figure out the best "in." Per Fey Standards of Conduct, the best way to torture relies on letting the subject choose their own pain as outcomes of their own failings (and I noticed with awe that you did that in your own posting "RE: Test/Extra Credit"—you are an inspiration!).

The subject's name is Josef. He has lived alone since his wife died giving birth to their only child. He is a sad, bereft man, and I know, I know—you said the lower someone starts, the harder it is to bring them to the depths. More fun to kick the world out from under someone when they are on top of a mountain.

But something about this one calls to me.

I must think on his challenge, and on what will happen to him in the end.

Any suggestions? I'm going to forget about even pretending not to cheat.

Oh, and speaking of… another list is attached. A few students I've heard badmouthing you. I obviously don't expect you to believe this based on nothing more than my word, so I have also included sound clips for your convenience.

Your student,

RG

Attachments: *culling.list.2.doc*
*WhyDoesOGetEverything.mp3*
*SomedayI'LLBeInCharge.mp3*
*WhatsHisIsReallyOurs-OrShouldBe.mp3*

—

DORM POSTING:

FROM: O

TO: ALL STUDENTS

RE: Students report to Me

The following eighteen students should report to Me immediately. I am pleased with your progress and, in the tradition of our People, those who please Me are rewarded.

[list follows on next page]

—

DORM POSTING:

FROM: O

TO: ALL STUDENTS

RE: Cleanup

Please suspend your projects for the next twelve hours. There are eighteen bodies hidden in The Wood. Find them and dispose of them in a way befitting My displeasure.

Some of the bodies will require more effort and ingenuity to find than others, due to those students' remains being spread liberally around The Wood in tiny chunks.

N.B.: this assignment *will* be part of your final grade.

—

FROM: RG@feyschool.edu

TO: O@feyschool.edu

My Dearest Professor O.,

Please enjoy the contents of the steamer trunks (sent with this letter).

I understand three other students managed to find bodies before I did. However, before you decide on marks for this part of the project, please note that the contents they shipped were *INTACT*.

Mine: not so much. You'll understand when you open the trunks, and I hope you enjoy the gifts I have sent.

Sincerely yours,

RG

P.S. I must congratulate you on an excellent job hiding the pieces! The skins, in particular, were hard to find. I had to capture Barghest, then train that infernal hound to hunt the scent of human skin, which I did by wrapping a few souls I had in my possession in several complete human skins I had earlier acquired in a game of unchance.

A lot of effort. But that made it all the more fun… and reassembling my once fellow students was a delight!

—

FROM: O@feyschool.edu

TO: RG@feyschool.edu

RG,

A personal note. Your assembling of the bodies was disgusting, depraved, disheartening, and inspired. Full marks!

I particularly liked how the pieces all came assembled, but into the wrong bodies. A patchwork quilt of corpses. It reminded Me of *The Modern Prometheus,* which has not been written yet, but which I recommend you read once our time has caught up to My Sight in that regard.

By the way: having two of these patchworks posed in what can only be described as an obscene (and, I would have thought, physiologically impossible) position was—to put it mildly—fantastic.

But, as always with our People, rewards come at a cost. I have, indeed, punished the three students who turned in the other bodies. You will be required to find their bodies as well, assemble them into similar delights, and return them to My office where I will keep them for the rest of the term, or for all eternity—whichever comes last.

You will not be granted a suspension of time to complete this task. It must be done simultaneously with the rest of your project.

I sincerely hope you have figured out what to do with your pitiful farmer, Josef. My Sight is eternal, but the time for this test wanes quickly.

- O.

—

FROM: RG@feyschool.edu

TO: O@feyschool.edu

Dear Professor O.,

I thought you would enjoy the following transcript of the first stage of my final exam project. I have written it out following the style of the theater, as I know you enjoy a good play.

Cordially,

RG

P.S. The three additional bodies are in your office. I dressed them so they all look as much like your wife as possible. None of them approach her beauty, but the resemblance is certainly there, and given the displeasure you must be feeling toward her after your recent child custody battle, I trust you will delight in watching the pale imitations of your queen as they rot. I have no idea how long that will actually take—how long does it last when a Partial Immortal dies, and its body becomes merely meat? —but it should prove enjoyable for you.

Speaking of which: if you don't mind, I would like to document the process. Not for any academic purpose. I just think it will be fun.

## "FINALE"

*ACT 1*

*A dusty hovel in the woods. A single room. A makeshift bed in a corner. A crib—empty—beside it.*

*TOOLS hang from one rough-hewn wall. They are old, rusty. Only one is in good repair: the sickle, whose razor edge gleams even in the dim light of the place.*

*A single candle burns low on the small table in the center of the room. There are two chairs beside it, though only one is occupied. JOSEF sits on it.*

*Josef is twenty-eight years old, but looks fifty, with haggard eyes and hollow, stubbled cheeks.*

*He eats dinner, glancing at the empty bed—big enough for two.*

*He does NOT look at the crib. Not ever.*

*The candle on the table FLICKERS.*

*A wind WHIPS through the windows, which are nothing but holes hacked in two of the walls. Josef shudders.*

JOSEF (stares at candle; crosses self) Good God, do take this misery from my heart. I do not deserve such pain. I deserve… *better.*

*The candle flickers again. The flames dance, and then turn into… a shape. Josef stares, mouth open as the flames slowly solidify into the outline of a woman.*

JOSEF Ana?

*The fire-Ana SPLITS, and now there are a man and a woman, dancing in the flame.*

*The woman of fire is beautiful, an idealized version of memory. The man, too. He is obviously modeled on Josef, but gone is the despair, the pain.*

*Josef smiles, delighted. Then the smile shatters as the woman in the flames crumbles, clutching her stomach. Her belly swells. She screams soundlessly.*

*The man in the flame—the Josef in the fire—watches her. He does not move to help, even as she reaches for him.*

*The fire-Josef waits. Waits. Then draws a knife. The flaming blade drops, plunging into her belly. More silent screams. Sparks fly like blood glittering in the night.*

JOSEF No!

*He swipes the candle off the table.*

—

FROM: O@feyschool.edu

TO: RG@feyschool.edu

RG,

I have received your project status update. I do enjoy plays, when they are well done. As for yours… I withhold judgment until the final grades.

- O.

—

FROM: RG@feyschool.edu

TO: O@feyschool.edu

Professor O.,

I totally understand.

Also, please see the photo attached. It might be of interest. Marvelous things, these "cameras"—I *am* sad we'll only be able to use technology from our own era post-graduation (unless, of course, any of us Ascend to the point where we may step outside of Time when it pleases us… ahhh, to dare to dream of such a thing!).

And re the photo, please remember: don't shoot the messenger!

All the best to you and yours,

RG

Attachment: *TheQueenAndHerLovers.jpg*

—

DORM POSTING:

FROM: O

TO: ALL (remaining) STUDENTS

RE: Lustful actions

Please be advised: the seven of you who took turns with My wife are… no longer able to do such things.

To the rest of you, I offer this advice: to attempt mischief is Fey, and expected. To be *caught* is sloppy, and unforgivable. Please see the painting on the next page. I am quite proud of it, as simultaneously castrating seven Fey while painting their pain was quite a challenge!

—

FROM: RG@feyschool.edu

TO: O@feyschool.edu

Prof,

Transcript of second act follows.

Cheers,

# <u>"FINALE"</u>

*ACT 2*

*The same dusty hovel. An air of desperation now permeates it.*

*Josef watches the candle. No telling how long he has sat thus, but where he had stubble before, now his face is covered by a beard. He has lost weight, and his eyes are sunken and blazing.*

*The candle still dances. He still sees himself murder his wife, over and over.*

JOSEF But it didn't happen that way. I loved you, Ana. I would never hurt you.

*Fire-Ana is being eviscerated by flame-Josef. And again. And again.*

*The fourth time, she reaches into the sparking gash created by flame-Josef. She pulls something out of herself.*

*Josef screams a mad scream at this newest obscenity.*

JOSEF (looking away) Stop! I don't deserve this!

*A voice, feminine but low, the voice of a lover, comes from the flame.*

FIRE-ANA But you do. You killed me. You gave me the *thing* that killed me.

*And now Josef realizes that, in looking away from the candle, his gaze has come to rest upon the empty crib.*

*Only… it is empty no more. A bundle inside it, visible through the slats. A twist of covers.*

*Something slides out of the covers. A hand, small, bloody.*

*A BABY cries.*

JOSEF It's not true! I didn't… I would do anything… I would give anything to have you back! (turning to Fire-Ana) To have you BOTH back!

FIRE-ANA Anything?

*She laughs, pulling out her insides as she does. Viscera fall from within her, disappearing in flame before touching the candle below her feet.*

*Sparks fly from the gaping gash. They transmute to blood mid-flight, and that blood now spatters Josef's cheeks and reddens the hands he has raised to cover his eyes.*

*Fire-Ana pulls out something small. Something that moves, like the thing in the crib moved.*

*Behind Josef, another cry—wet, rough, like a babe shrieking through a mouthful of dirt and blood—pierces the night.*

JOSEF (a hoarse, haunted whisper). Anything.

*The candle winks out. Darkness, absolute and deep.*

*The baby cries again, an unseen thing in a crib that was empty and should be empty still.*

JOSEF (in the dark). Anything at all.

—

FROM: O@feyschool.edu

TO: RG@feyschool.edu

RG,

I must admit, I enjoyed the second part of your final exam. The gift basket that accompanied it was a nice touch. Though two of the muffins had a bite taken out of them… what the *hell* were you thinking, profaning My gift basket like that?

- O.

—

FROM: RG@feyschool.edu

TO: O@feyschool.edu

Big O.,

I *am* glad you enjoyed the second act.

Sorry about the muffins! I have no idea how that happened. The basket was delivered by my two best friends—you know the ones, they sit on either side of me during class—and they *are* both famously lacking in self-control (especially when it comes to food). But I'm sure they didn't eat the muffins. Totally sure. More than half sure. Mostly.

Sorta.

Good news, though: my final exam project is complete!

Peace out!

RG

—

FROM: O@feyschool.edu

TO: RG@feyschool.edu

RG,

Your friends are dead. I wanted you to know, and I wanted you to hear it from Me.

I interrogated both (the thought that you had framed them *did* cross My mind; that would be a very Fey thing to do) with some… ahem… *enthusiasm,* so I am quite sure both told Me the truth. As My rage at losing the gift basket to their lack of self-control had been piqued, I determined that the best response to their taking a bite of My muffins was to let them feel the same pain. So, I took bites of *them.* I started delicately, of course; their eyes were delicious. The noses and ears were chewy but serviceable, but their tongues—sugar-coated by countless years of lies and flatteries in service of their desires—were the perfect *digestif.*

I could continue with the details, but fear I might wax so enthusiastic that it would bore you. Suffice it to say that by the time I had gotten around to removing the kidneys from both their bodies and frying them up in pans made of the tops of their own skulls, both died.

I was quite disappointed at the lack of strength that showed.

At any rate, do not think for one moment that grief will give you an excuse for turning in the results of your final project. Late reports or incomplete projects merit a failing grade on their face, and well… I don't have to tell you what happens then, do I? Only that nothing that has happened thus far will hold the merest candle to the punishment that will be meted out in such a case.

- O.

P.S. Don't think I haven't noticed the continuing degradation of your salutations. They started out barely serviceable, and have become utterly disrespectful. I honestly don't understand what a bright student like you is thinking, addressing Me like that, but in this as in all things, there will be a reckoning.

—

FROM: RG@feyschool.edu

TO: O@feyschool.edu

What up, homey?

Please see attached: the third act of my final exam.

See you at my graduation! ;o)

RG

"FINALE"

*ACT 3*

*The hovel. It appears as though a tornado has hit it: the effects of the frenzy that has overtaken its owner.*

*He tries to light the candle, using a flint and steel. No matter how hard he tries, it will not catch.*

JOSEF Ana! Ana, where are you? Come back to me! I want you. I need you! I *deserve you!*

*At this last, a sound. The flame still does not catch, but a cooing comes from the bed. The sound of a child content.*

*Before Josef can turn to it, the candle sputters.*

FIRE-ANA (from the sputtering flame, though she is not seen) Some things should not be, my love.

*Josef's expression becomes a rictus of rage.*

JOSEF No. You cannot do that! You cannot show yourself to me, then take away the promise of your return!

FIRE-ANA (still unseen) But we are all allotted a time. I had mine. A good time, a time—

JOSEF (spittle flying) *I WILL HAVE YOU! I DESERVE MORE! I DESERVE BETTER!*

FIRE-ANAThen…

*The flame sputters once, then dies. The cooing comes from the bed again.*

*Josef turns to it. He goes to it, staring down at what is bundled there.*

*For a moment, it seems he sees the mangled remains of a child.*

*Then the child is gone. In its place: the razor-sharp sickle.*

*Josef draws it from the bed. Madness lights flames in his eyes, the flames dancing like the images of his wife and child in the candle.*

FIRE ANA (still unseen, her voice now sounding throughout the hovel, everywhere and nowhere at once) You want us back…

JOSEF Yes. I deserve to have you. You are mine, the baby is mine, you…

*As he speaks, Josef draws the sickle across his belly. Blood wells thick and red.*

JOSEF … are…

*He reaches inside. Pulling out what he finds in rolling masses.*

JOSEF … all…

*The floor is stained with Josef's own bowels. Some of it falls in the crib itself, a grim parody of the life that never lay there, the visions that were seen.*

JOSEF … *mine*!

*There is nothing more inside him. Nothing more to find, nothing to hold.*

*Josef falls.*

*Darkness.*

*A moment later, the candle sputters to life. Laughter can be heard from within it.*

THE END

—

DORM POSTING:

FROM: O

TO: RG

RE: Final grade and addenda

This is addressed to a single student. Normally, the process for a final exam to see who is advanced to Full Fey status involves a final separation of the wheat from the chaff. Two or three are chosen, the rest destroyed.

With the recent destruction of the two students who ate My muffins, there is only one student remaining to receive a grade at all; hence My addressing this final memo only to you.

A breakdown of your project follows.

Suitability of subject: It was not lost on Me that the farmer was a greedy type—evidenced by the sharpness of his tools but their otherwise lackluster condition; he obviously wanted to reap a grand harvest, but at the same time was unwilling to do all the work necessary for such, the hallmark of the truly greedy. I also noticed his language, though apparently rooted in grief, was eventually revealed as the wording of someone who thinks they "deserve" it all.PASS.

Performance: Your performance—both as the wife in the flame and as the baby—were excellent. But there was little of them. Less *is* more, but I would have liked to see your hand a bit more often and less subtly, if only for purposes of the exam.FAIL.

Final consequences: Again, it was good as far as it went. There was a nice balance to the fact that, in seeking to have the ultimate benefit, the undeserving farmer eventually tried to find the object of his greed within himself—and died for it. That said, the setup and payoff were too obvious, and not nearly creative enough. Being boring is a criminal offense among our kind.FAIL

OVERALL GRADE: **FAIL**

The above notwithstanding, I realized (at the very moment when I was going to dispatch the Hunters to find you) that you had, in fact, done more than it, at first, appeared. It is a tenet that the punishments must fit the crime, and at first I thought you had simply repaid the farmer's greed appropriately.

Then I realized:

Eighteen students were destroyed for Sloth (fifteen who chose the safety of The Wood in case of failure; three who turned in bodies but failed to do anything interesting with them).

Three were destroyed for their Envy (the ones you reported who coveted after My stature and position).

Seven were destroyed for Lust (those who had their way with My wife, who even now suffers as well, though the details of her suffering are private as befitting her station).

Two were destroyed for Gluttony (I hope their taste of forbidden muffins was worth it).

And, of course, Josef was destroyed for his Greed.

Which leaves only Pride and Wrath.

The former belongs to you. Your salutations went from barely respectful enough to pass muster, to those one might see in communiques between peers, to greetings as of a friend to another. As though we held the same station. There was further Pride in the fact that you felt comfortable manipulating the test for your own ends, and in your irregular updates, indicating that you felt yourself beyond the rules of the test.

And, of course, the Pride shown by your assumption that you would graduate and be awarded Full Fey status.

And as for Wrath… it is Mine. You have done so much to deserve it, My young student, and many were the ways of pain I had devised for you. Only Pride, as the greatest of the sins, deserves so much more than mere torture unto dissolution. And, ultimately, My Wrath compels Me to issue the following:

4) OVERALL GRADE: **~~FAIL~~ PASS**

Were you not Fully Fey, your Immortality would be limited and, like the rest of the students in your class, I could destroy you—leisurely, and with great pleasure. But as much as I would enjoy it, and as many agonizing delights as I had prepared for you in My mind, all must eventually needs end.

Unless you graduated. Because at the graduation ceremony, you will become Full Fey, and so Fully Immortal.

In other words: you are Mine for eternity. And great will be your suffering. You, the student with more Pride than any I have ever seen in all My long eons, you impudent hobgoblin, will be brought lower than the dust, and then lower still.

You have won your status. Enjoy it… I know I will.

- O.

# Grounded

Patti Larsen

I shouldn't be surprised to find myself on my backside on the hardwood floor, but somehow, I am. I choke on the billowing smoke coming from the beaker now overflowing with nasty green foam and wait for the miasma of revolting disgustingness to dissipate. At least I can hear Reggie coughing from his side of the room, so I know not to be too concerned.

He's alive, at least.

I make it to the window, heave it open with a desperate, concentrated thought. Funny how I still reach for things physically, even though I haven't been able to actually touch most objects for over a decade. That kind of habit just doesn't die.

Fresh air does its duty, wafting the hideous cloud of lingering failure out into the yard. Good thing his room backs onto the garden so no one's the wiser. By the time the smoke is gone, I'm feeling better. Sure, despite the fact I'm for all intents and purposes (mostly) non corporeal, I'm still effected by anything to do with the contents of the box on the desk.

My whole life is in that little box.

With lungs aching like someone shoveled burning coal down my throat, I turn to check on the cause of all this mess. Considering Reggie's track record with such experiments, all that matters is we're in one piece.

Well, technically not true. But he divested me of what rests in that little box a long time ago, so one piece is relative.

"You okay?" His muffled groan of assent precedes Reggie's appearance. He somehow ended up on the other side of his bed, the ruffled quilt evidence he'd bounced rather aggressively over the soft surface. A blessing he had it to break his fall.

"Been better." He flips his broken glasses aside, unable to see through the shattered lenses, faint British accent as much a part of him as the cowlick in the front of his dark hair, untamable and even more unruly thanks to the recent blast. "You?"

I shrug join him, helping him to his feet. Ironic the only person I can touch is the person who put me in this position in the first place. I've given up on blaming Reggie, though. Mostly.

"I guess it didn't work then," I say. I don't have to fake it to keep the disappointment from my voice. I'm used to failure after almost fifteen years of trying.

Reggie refuses to let it get him down, however. And this time is no exception.

"Just have to tweak the formula." He is already off in his own little world, staggering to the bench and his chemicals, smudge of green goo on his cheek, speckling his shirt. He's too tiny and fragile looking to tolerate such abuse as regularly as he does. "I'm sure we were close. Did you feel anything?"

I want to tell him yes. I've done so in the past, lied about the possibility of success just to give him some respite from the guilt that eats him from the inside like a disease. I see it now in his dark brown eyes, in his earnest expression, how his little hands clench into fists against my answer.

Lying in the past has only ever brought both of us heartache. Being honest? Might sting in the moment, but it's preferable to crushing him when he finds out the truth.

"Sorry," I say, joining him at the bench, averting my eyes from the contents of the box. I can't bear to look at them at times like this, so soon after another attempt to reattach what he plucked from between my shoulder blades when he was just a toddler.

"I'm sorry, Petal," he says, mournful today. Some days he's chipper, excited to try again. But mostly his sorrow and regret are pretty much expected.

"It's okay, Reg." How many times have I reassured him in the past? "We'll figure it out. You'll see."

My usual reassurance falls flat, even to me. Before I can try again, his fingertips drum on the surface of the table, brow creased while he reaches into his desk cubby for a fresh pair of glasses. His parents have stopped asking how he breaks so many. And he only blows things up when they aren't home. We learned that they don't care, in their wealthy English prim and properness, what he's up to as long as he doesn't burn the house down.

Or talk about his imaginary friend. Ahem.

"I'll make it right." He stands, faces me, eyes liquid, jaw tight. Reaches for me, touches my hand, memory burning between us—

*—the tiny human, adorable, giggling, cups me in his hand. I'm fascinated. He feels different, unique, familiar. Why does this human feel like family? It's my first time interacting with one of their young, the only safe time to investigate mortals. Before they grow up and forget we're real, we fairies.*

*He's equally absorbed in me, other hand reaching out. I hear her calling my name, but it's too late, my mother too far, her warning coming the instant his fingers close on the sparkling, rainbow beauty of my wings—*

I shudder, drop Reggie's hand, gaze falling, unbidden, to the box on the table. It doesn't always happen when I touch him, but the recall of that moment, the instant his two-year-old self pulled off my wings, aches every time it surfaces.

Like a loss I'll never recover from.

I stare at them, to the naked mortal eye simply a pair of tiny, pressed leaves, long dried but still perfect. To me? They glow, that iridescence reminding me of who I used to be.

Sorrow encompassing both of us, our shared despair palpable because we've lived it together for so long, Reggie takes pity and closes the box.

"Reggie, darling pet." Mary's into her second martini already, her own accent precision London, though they've lived here in the States for almost twenty years. I can see the alcohol in her system in the muddle aura around her, Reggie's mother seated at the dining room table, her slim body achingly tiny in the giant room, dark paneled walls oppressive despite the towering ceiling and sparkling chandelier doing its best to light the space.

Archie is face-deep in his evening paper, tipping the corner to nod to his son before going back to his business section. "We have company. Come kiss your Great Auntie Fay."

I hadn't noticed the old woman, her broad face deeply crevassed by time and bad genetics. But there's nothing feeble about her and, while my friend makes his uncomfortable way to his great aunt's side, I share in his lack of enthusiasm. There's something off about her, creepy. It's only when Reggie leans in, the old woman's big hands grasping the sides of his face and squishing his cheeks for a solid kiss, I realize what it is about her that gives me the willies.

She's without an aura. Not a hint of life to speak of.

I shudder a little and back off a step, though at the same time sending out a bit of magic to envelop Reggie. I don't have much power left, not since losing my wings, but for some reason protecting him has always come easily to me.

Auntie Fay smiles up at him, beady black eyes glinting from folds of powder-white skin, lipstick running into the cracks around her thick mouth. She had to choose that shade of red that made her look as though she's been feeding on flesh with abandon, didn't she?

"Dear Reginald," Auntie Fay says, voice deep, graveled, two-packs-a-day though I don't sense that habit about her. "I haven't seen you since you were a babe in nappies."

"Auntie." Reggie clearly has no memory of her, the magic connecting us expanding in response to my discomfort. He's at a loss for words. I prod him with the power I hold, making him twitch, breaking him from the frozen state of *don't touch me* that holds him enthralled. Classic introvert, poor kid.

She releases him when he physically tugs himself out of her grasp, her big hands settling with two meaty thunks on the armrests of her dining chair. Reggie circles the table, taking a seat next to his father, about as far from Auntie Fay as possible. I hover behind him, knowing there's not much I can do to help except be here for him.

Small comfort, but the best I can do.

"Your mother tells me you've shown an aptitude for the sciences." Mary nods enthusiastically as the black and white clad maid refills her quickly emptied martini.

"He's an absolute delight," his mother gushes before kicking her husband under the table. "Isn't he, Archie, dear heart?"

Reggie's father grunts, lowers his paper, blinking pale blue eyes behind his wire rim glasses, tie loosened but never removed. I've only ever seen Archie in his three-piece suit, in various stages of business readiness. "Indeed, Mary, my love." His enthusiasm for the conversation satisfied, he returns to his paper.

Auntie Fay doesn't seem to care. "Are you all over that silly imaginary friend business?"

Mary chokes on her drink, Archie's paper shuddering when he finally gives the visitor his full attention.

"Not for years and years now," he says in that clipped and professional way of his that says this topic is closed and she'd be well put to mind her own business, thank you very much.

But Auntie Fay is smiling at Reggie, if you can call that grotesque grimace a smile and, through my power's contact with him, I feel him softening. It's not often he's on the business end of anyone's heart-felt approval. All the *my loves* and *darling dears* can't replace actual affection.

Far be it for me to judge his parents. I'm just a wingless fairy forced to endure the consequences of their parenting.

"It was just a phase." Reggie's discomfort returns as he lies. He's not good at it, never has been, looks down at his plate while the serving girl sets a salad in front of him, Archie already setting aside his paper to devour what's in front of him. Mary ignores hers in favor of a drink refill, Aunt Fay inhaling hers with gusto. "Therapy helped."

I'd attended said therapy with him, mostly out of boredom since Reggie's the only person who can see me. Or, at least, the only person who will interact with me. Other fairies can, I know it, but when they spot me they just run away. So it's him or nothing.

I don't want to think about what happens when he's gone. I've got decades, I hope. And, maybe he will find a way to reattach my wings.

Not holding my breath.

I lean in and help myself to a leaf from Reggie's plate. Not that I have to eat, but vegetation is one of the only things I can make easy physical contact with, and chewing gives me something to do.

In the moment I touch the spinach leaf, it vanishes.

And Auntie Fay reacts.

It's subtle, the faintest twitch, come and gone in a flutter. I'm not even sure it happened at all, it's over so fast. I stare at her, wondering, while Mary speaks, words slurring just a little as her genteel ways are overcome by the vermouth and gin.

"All that's behind us. Reggie's showing an aptitude for science, Auntie, did I tell you?" That sad and haunted look on her face, the one she reserves for her only son? I wish I knew what it meant.

Dinner with the family. Always a prim and proper train wreck.

Reggie flips on the light and closes his door behind him, leaning against it, that forlorn and unhappy expression he always wears when forced to spend dinner with his parents engulfing him a moment. It's late, after 10PM. Usually they take pity and let him leave after dinner, before Mary's fully overcome by her drinking. It's gotten worse over the years, though there's not much we can do about it. I've tried magic, at Reggie's request. Somehow, when my power touches her, it only makes things worse.

Tonight his mother lingered, even if Archie made his own retreat. Mary's imbibing didn't slow, Auntie Fay's tolerance admirable, Reggie's misery a weight between us until his mother's limit for alcohol was finally, epically, reached and she bid her son and visitor a tottering good night.

The way she kisses him when she's that drunk gives me frequent pause. How she looks in his eyes as if searching for something she's lost, her lower lip trembling, her breath caught. Always makes me wonder what it is she's seeking.

I just wish I could ask her.

"I love you, my darling dear," she slurred finally, questioning look shuttered behind inebriation, before weaving her uncertain way to the door.

Reggie took that as his chance to exit and bolted before Auntie Fay could ask for another kiss. Smart boy.

I touch his hand where he stands, back pressed to the heavy wood of his door, the power still between us, distracting him. Not really for his benefit, mind you. Even without magic connecting us his moods tend to reach me regardless. And while I have the option to wall him off, he's all I have. I'm all he has.

Doesn't seem fair to cut him off when everyone else in his life chooses to.

Reggie sinks to his bed, hands folded behind his head, staring at the ceiling. I perch on his office chair, swinging back and forth, just enough contact with the hardwood floor under my bare feet to give me the physical contact necessary to swivel. Frustrating and satisfying in equal measure, though it takes a lot of effort to do even this much.

"Petal." Reggie sounds like he's on the verge of tears. I forget sometimes he's only seventeen, despite his diminutive stature, his frailty. Then again, I'm not much older. But he acts ancient, far more than the teens I've observed on television with him when he chooses to waste an hour or so on what he calls trivial time. His brilliance is honestly the only thing that gives me hope he might succeed someday in fixing what he did so long ago.

"Reggie." I echo his tone exactly, hoping for a grin from him, a lightening of mood.

Instead, he sighs, turns his head, overhead light catching the lenses of his glasses, blocking the view of his dark eyes. "When you get your wings back, will you take me with you?"

He's never mentioned anything of the sort before. "Where?"

Well, that's pretty obvious, isn't it? The fairy realm.

Reggie sits up, elbows on his knees, face in his hands. "I can't anymore, Petal. I don't belong here."

I don't get to answer. Someone knocks on the door, startling both of us.

Reggie's on his feet and moving, answering the summons. I stand back, discomfort returning, while he greets his visitor. Auntie Fay looms in the light of the hallway outside his room, towering over him, blocky body crammed into a flowered dress that barely contains her bulk. I find myself staring in awe at the size of her feet and those massive, comfortable-looking beige shoes she wears as she speaks.

"May I come in?"

Reggie lets her, of course he does. He's a good boy, isn't he? She enters, looks around, smiles at his chemistry desk, the science books. Pauses and lingers over the chronicles he's found over the years, the leather-bound volumes on his bookshelf, all about fairies.

"You mustn't let them trouble you, dear Reggie," Auntie Fay says, thick fingers drifting over the spines of those books. He's read everything—most of it bunk—about my people. I might have been young when I was forced out by my loss, but fae memory filled in the gaps. Everything he can find, that is. She doesn't seem surprised by his choice of reading material. "You're special, my pet. You always have been."

Reggie doesn't say a word, hands clasped behind his back, watching her circle his room. She returns to the chemistry work station again, those curious fingers touching everything. I want to tell her to stop, to mind her own business, but there's not much I can do except watch and engulf Reggie in power to protect him.

From what?

I don't know. But my instincts are screaming and I can't help myself.

Auntie Fay's hand hovers over *the box*—leave it *alone*, don't touch my *wings*—a moment before she turns and smiles at Reggie, her bulk shifting toward him. He starts, steps back, trips over the end of his bed, catches himself even as my magic helps. Clumsy, always clumsy. I hold him firmly in my power until he rights himself.

"Perhaps we can talk further tomorrow." She seems concerned by his reaction, doesn't try to touch him or hug him, thankfully, instead nodding and heading for the exit. Reggie looks as relieved as I feel and I drift behind him, one hand on his shoulder in support, while he jerks open the door, staring up at her with huge eyes behind his glasses.

"Let's." He blurts that one word like it's all he can manage.

Auntie Fay smiles again, grimace of threat meant to reassure, I'm certain, but only increasing his discomfort. Reggie's shaking under my touch.

"Good night then, dear," she says. Her gaze flickers over his shoulder.

To me.

And then she's gone, the door firmly shut behind her, while Reggie gasps out the breath he's clearly been holding far too long. All the while my insides flip over and over and a terrible anxious sensation bubbles deep within.

"That was the weirdest—" Reggie goes silent when I spin from him, rush to the desk. Search for what I already know is missing, that anxiety turning to panic.

"The box," I whispered. "My wings."

Reggie gapes, his own horror connecting with mine.

"They're gone."

Easier for me to sneak than for Reggie, but he manages. He knows this house as well as I do, after all. The two of us have spent countless hours wandering the halls, exploring the many crannies, the darkened nooks, entertaining ourselves in the dim and musty corridors where only history whispers, where I'm sure feet haven't met carpet aside from the maids and their endless cleaning for decades.

It's not hard to figure out which room Auntie May has been relegated to. Has to be east wing, second floor, likely two or three doors down from Mary, at least as far from Archie. I pass Reggie's mother's room, the sound of her snoring penetrating even the heavy wood of her suite's stately double doors and I don't wonder why her husband, his matching chainsaw mimic across the hall, chose to escape to his own set of rooms.

It has always seemed to me a sad way to live, but what do I know?

I expend a little magic, trying to find my wings. It's not that they call to me. Kind of the opposite, in fact. There's a rather empty feeling to them despite the fact they belong to me. Though, I'd never admit as much to Reggie, I worry about that lack of connection to them. Have the rejected me somehow? Or, does the missing, absent feeling of them, that void of where they should be—whether between my shoulder blades or in the box where they've rested all these years—mean they don't actually belong to me anymore?

Does the fact they seem to have rejected me and any attempt to reattach them equate to me fighting a fate I really just need to accept already?

I'd voice it, but Reggie… he'd never forgive himself. And he's my only source of companionship. Can't have him falling apart on me over guesswork and maybes.

Case in point. He's intently focused on our task, pausing to listen at each doorway past where his parents compete in their current Snoring Wars. I wish I can be of more help, drifting from door to door behind him, not feeling—or, not *not* feeling—that vacant emptiness that would mean my wings reside on the other side.

Reggie pauses at last, turns a knob, slips into a room and I join him. He's chosen correctly, it seems, a large wheelie suitcase parked in one corner of the bedroom past the small sitting area, though the bed itself is empty, perfectly made, the bag unpacked, as though the visitor who'd brought it had no intention of staying.

"She came here looking for my wings." It was the only logical conclusion.

Reggie shot me a look over his shoulder, frowning, skinny body tense. "How would she know? And why? What reason could she possibly have to want them? They're useless." Reggie flinches as though realizing what he's said. "To her, I mean," he covers quickly.

I don't comment because what's the point, really? "Her things are still here," I say. "She has to come back for them eventually." All the while, she's somewhere as yet unidentified with my wings, doing who-knew-what with them.

"Maybe she doesn't know what she took." Reggie doesn't sound convinced.

"Or maybe she knew exactly what she was after," I say, hating to repeat myself but not sure he's understanding the gravity of this situation, "and I'll never see my wings again." Eep. Was that a wail of despair in my voice? Reggie shivers and I quickly pull myself under control. Excessive emoting makes my power unpredictable. I'd even been known to clear a room when something made me cry.

"It's okay, Petal." Reggie's jaw sets, face creased, adding years to his appearance. "We'll find her. Let's keep looking."

It's been hard, I admit, all these years, knowing my wings were right there in that wooden box in Reggie's possession. I couldn't use them, couldn't make them return to me, but there were *there*. There's always been something comforting about that fact, despite the predicament I've ended up in.

This is the first time I've had to come face-to-face with certain truths that poke me with tiny, painful fingers as I follow Reggie on his search through the house. His sneakers make less sound on the plush carpeting than my heart does in my own ears while panic grows, encompasses, devours me. By the time we've thoroughly combed the entire mansion from one end to the other, including the west wing, twice no less, despair has taken over.

I'm near weeping when Reggie finally turns to me and grasps me firmly by the shoulders. He's been silent the last little while, his back to me while I wallowed in my growing sorrow, tumbling down into the darkness of accepting I'll never be whole again.

As for Reggie, his face is sheathed in tears, dark eyes pink around the edges, nose running while he shakes me just a little, clearing his throat. "Petal," he whispers, hoarse. "Please. Stop. I can't take any more and if you keep going we'll never find your wings because I swear I'm going to curl up in a ball and cry my eyes out."

Snap. I hug him, a rare show of weakness on my part. Why I think showing him affection is weakness I'm not certain, but it's typically unnatural. Right now? It's the only thing I can do. We cling to each other a long moment while the grandfather clock downstairs in the main foyer, just a few doors and the sweeping staircase away, tolls five times.

"It's almost dawn," he says, his own resignation growing. Why the coming of morning makes things seem more final I have no idea.

Until, in a flicker of magic, I feel something I haven't in fifteen years.

"Reggie." I gasp his name, grasping his hand, turning this way and that, trying to get a location from that aching sensation now prodding the middle of my back. Demanding, that feeling, commanding. I drag him, unable to stop myself, heading, not for the room Auntie Fay was assigned, but to the back of the house. The wide, marble steps leading into the garden.

The same garden where, at two years old, Reggie changed my life forever.

"Something's happening." I glance over my shoulder at him. He nods to me, just visible in the darkness of the garden. Climbing bushes and fruit trees line paths through the space, past statues and a single fountain in the center. The tugging is stronger now, almost jerking me off my feet, Reggie running alongside me.

It stops as suddenly as it started and I skid to a halt, at the outer edge near the low stone wall that marks the boundary of the property. Something dark looms in the near black, turns slowly, ponderously, revealing as it does the sparkling light of my furiously beating wings.

That light illuminates a familiar face, though only barely recognizable now. Auntie Fay's bulbous nose has taken on epic proportions, her sloping brow sharp edged, as though carved from rock. The flowered dress she wore is torn in places, her mass seemingly doubled since our last encounter.

"Troll," I whisper.

"Half," she says, that voice unchanged at least. "My mother was human."

"You can see her?" Poor Reggie. So flummoxed.

"She can," I say. "Has all along. Haven't you, Auntie Fay? In fact, you've known I've been here since the beginning. Since Reggie took my wings."

She doesn't answer, but there's no need. Instead, she shifts her stance, now massive toes digging into the soil. My wings flap in angry protest, the tug from them returning in a jab of agony that drives me to my knees.

"Give them back," I whisper. "Please. They don't belong to you."

Auntie Fay closes her massive hand over them, crushing them into silence. No, not completely. Sparkles fall from her grip, tumbling in angry tinkles to the ground while she fights to keep her fingers firmly in place. "You have no idea, child," she says.

"You're a monster," Reggie says then, challenge in his voice. What's he planning to do? Take on a troll? Half troll. Even half of her is far more than either of us can handle.

She laughs then, guttural and akin to the sound of two rocks being ground together. "I am," she says. Points at me with her free hand, my eyes adjusted back to the blackness sufficiently I can follow her movements. "So is she." Auntie Fay pauses, levels her index finger, the thickness of a tree root, at Reggie. "And so, my dear Reggie, are you."

Neither of us expected that. I reach for his hand, feel him reject my attempt to deny her statement through touch, stepping away from me. Shoulders back, head high, faint light catching his glasses as the barest touch of dawn woke in the east. "What are you talking about?" His voice doesn't shake. And, frankly, I know him well enough to know he isn't surprised.

Isn't surprised at all.

"Changeling," Auntie Fay says, cruel joy in her gravel voice.

There's no denying it the instant the word is spoken. I turn to him, take in the familiar line of his jaw, how those ears arch just a bit too much to a point. Slim, short, slender. Unruly hair, small hands. Like me, delicate seeming. But it's not his appearance that seals it for me.

"Mary," I whisper. "She knows."

"She suspects something isn't right with her darling Reggie," Auntie Fay says. "The night I traded her human child for you, changeling, she woke as I was leaving. I felt her heart break. She may not be fae, but she has the sight, enough it torments her and has since I stole your namesake away three days and three nights after his birth."

Ritual, those three days and three nights. I know it like it's part of me. "It's why she drinks."

"She can't live with the truth," Auntie Fay says, stoic, flat. "Can't allow it to come to light. And so, she drowns in it. All the while waiting for her child to come home."

Something he'll never do. The fae don't give children back.

"Why my wings?" I can feel them fighting her even now. They've woken to me, reconnected at least in their anger. They feel like a separate entity and that sensation only reinforces my fears they will never again be mine. But I can't help but claim them in my heart. "Why now if you've known they were here all along? That I was?"

She lifts her fist to her chest, the sparkles dying out as a glow begins under her hand. "I'm running low on power," she says, "too long in the human world. I need them to continue my work."

"Stealing children for the fae," I say.

Again, no answer. Again, no need. I already know what she'd say. Because I'm like her.

I realize suddenly I can see far more than I could just a moment ago, the coming dawn staining the sky behind me, light casting over Auntie Fay. She's more hideous illuminated, though less frightening. Jagged, those folds of flesh that weren't quite, two shining black marbles for her eyes. All cold stone, she is, beneath that now tattered flower dress as the glow against her chest turns green, then silver, the power of my wings absorbed into her in a last gasp of magic stolen.

"Ah," she says, smiling, a truly hideous expression. "Just what Auntie needed."

Does she sense it, as she shifts? Does she know what's happening to her as her body expands, transforms, reshapes? I see her evolve, watch her with astonishment while the human in her fades completely, full troll taking her over while the sun clears the edge of the world and shines on all three of us.

She has an instant of understanding, mouth falling open to reveal blunt teeth, an "O" protest forming, freezing in place when the warmth of morning finds her, no longer half anything, but fully troll, and, as is its way, turns her to stone.

Neither of us move for a long time, the sun fully cleared the horizon by the time Reggie sighs.

"I guess that's the problem with fae magic," he says. "Even when you're fae yourself."

Tricky stuff, that. Be careful what you wish for.

I approach her slowly, heart aching, terrified of what I'll find. I'll have to shatter her hand in order to free my wings, if they even exist anymore. Likely the power that remained to them is gone and I'm truly stuck here, between worlds, forever.

Something flutters to the ground, settles. Sparkles briefly. Falls still. I kneel, gather the two dried leaves that are my wings into my hands and kiss them, one at a time.

While the power between us wakes, at least for a moment, before falling still again.

Hope. They are mine. I am theirs. And one day, one day, we will be whole again.

I look up, see Reggie squinting at Auntie Fay, the hulking troll frozen now for all time. He sighs, shakes his head, shrugs. But when he speaks, it's not to talk about the truths he's discovered, about my wings, about any of that momentous reveal that we'll have to sort out eventually. There's so much more to this than either of us ever understood.

Instead, he meets my eyes, his earnest behind the shining lenses of his glasses.

"Maybe Mum and Father won't notice we have a new statue."

I laugh. It seems the only appropriate thing to do.

# Purr, My Lovely

Sarah A. Hoyt

When the dame came into my office, she was all legs.

No, really, from my vantage point, low to the ground in front of my desk, all I could see was her legs, going up to a colored triangle under her tent-like skirt.

I twitched my whiskers. Most humans were all legs to us cats. We saw them in other ways. In this case, to my senses, she smelled young and scared and tired: very, very tired.

"What's up, Toots?" I told her.

Only I didn't really tell her. Look, I don't know what the chances are of a crazy 30s experiment trying to create tamable cats who could act as scouts for the army ending up, instead, with … in early twenty-first century terms, uplifted cats, with human intelligence. But I know the chances of changing a cat's mouth so it can pronounce human words are even lower than that.

So, even if the first happened and produced my ancestors, the second was unlikely.

In a pinch, when our other form of communication failed utterly, we, the Protectors, could talk. Sort of. For a limited form of speech. Sometimes our efforts ended up in the human's social media, and our nonsense words were made much fun of.

Only they were never nonsense. It's just that humans are sadly limited creatures. They don't know what's out there. They don't even know what's all around them on Earth. They're deaf, dumb, blind and think themselves masters of the universe.

If they weren't so cute, it would be kinder to put them out of their misery. It's just that we Protectors owe them a debt of sorts. Without them, we'd never have been what we are, never able to do the things we do. Oh, and yeah, they are cute.

So, we do what we can.

To me, what I could was be a PI, with an office in downtown Goldport, Colorado. Into which this young human female had come.

And I was speaking to her the way we speak to most humans. In their minds. Telepathy? I don't know. I'm not even sure how they define that these days. I do know that cats were always able to reach into human minds and play with their feelings, their emotions, and perhaps their thoughts. We, Protectors, did the same only more so.

So, what I'd thought in the girl's general direction was "greeting suitable for a young female and circumstances." What she heard was "What's up, Toots." Probably because we were in my second-floor office, in a 1930s building, with a pizza parlor on the bottom. And I was a PI.

Okay, that explanation above is almost complete nonsense. It's not that there weren't words in what I thought at her. It's more that our concept of words—

Never mind. There are things I can't tell across species. From here on out, I'll pretend I just talked to her, in words, as humans do. I am assured by my human pets that this is how they experience it. I'm assured, also, that I have a deep and masculine voice, with a slightly flippant, irreverent tone.

Which explains why she took a step backward, startled, and looked around wildly.

"Down here," I said, and as her eyes came to focus on me, I twitched my moustaches and did my best "imitation of human smile" look. Then I jumped on the desk, and said, "I believe this will be more comfortable for you. Mithra Tamuras de Shangrila, at your service."

She stayed quiet for a while, opening and closing her mouth like a newly landed fish. "Oh," she said at last, and it seemed like it took her entire concentration to say that. "You are a cat."

I am, to be exact, a very handsome orange tabby—my pets tell me—with an apple head and clear golden eyes. Not that it matters to other cats, or even other Protectors. We evaluate each other in different ways. But it was good to know that the humans considered me beautiful. It helped.

Yes, it also helped—and many of the other Protectors, in other towns and even in this one, working in other capacities, did it—to have a human act as a front for you, so that you spoke through him and such. There are many such partnerships. A lot of scientists, composers and writers are really just fronts for their cats. Reading Shakespeare, I've often wondered—But of course, it's nonsense, unless our descendants invent time travel.

Sure, one of my pets could stand in for me, but what I did was already so unbelievable and unlikely, it was easier to deal with the clients if they accepted me as I was.

"Well, yes. Mostly," I said. "Or perhaps ancestrally would be more accurate."

She seemed to lose all ability to stand, looked around, located the two chairs I kept for clients, and more or less dropped into one.

From this vantage point, with me now on top of the desk, and her sitting down, I could tell you she was attractive for a human. And yes, of course, I know what attractive is for a human. Protectors had been living with humans for almost a hundred years. That's potentially—although Protectors are longer lived than normal cats and tend to mate later and more rarely—a hundred of our generations, but really, for us, let's say fifty. That's in human terms as long ago as the sixth century. Of course, over that time we came to see what humans would like. I could describe her in Protector terms, but Protectors will have read my report filed with our organization. You're more than likely a human reading this, so I'll describe her in human terms: slight, blond, with curves in the right places, and big green eyes. The big green eyes looked too reflective, as if she'd been crying.

The emotions I sensed from her were confusion, and some embarrassment. As though there were something wrong with coming to me for help. From her point of view, probably, there was. I mean, she probably thought of me as a cat, just a cat.

She took a deep breath. "I can't believe that—"

"That you're coming to a cat for help. Only I'm not a cat, Toots. Not really. I'm about as much like your average pussycat as you're like a tree shrew. I'm a Protector."

She shook her head and swallowed. "My friend Marcy said to come to you. She said there was a ghost in her house and you—"

"Yeah. That's what we do. Myself and others like me." I groomed my left paw as I talked. I don't know why, but my middle claw always seems a little off, and there were tiny droplets of my lunch's blood in the fur. "We protect humanity from the things they can't see. The things they're not sure about. You know how common housecats stare at walls? We see… other places."

She frowned. "What kind of other places?"

"Places you don't want to see, sister," I said. "No, trust me. There are things in this world humans don't want to know about." And that was true, even when not knowing those things could kill them. Because the monkey brain only has so much space. Those who go hunting the supernatural tend to go insane in short order. Too much information coming at them all the time, short-circuiting their ability to process.

I yawned. "So, what's your problem? Ghosts?"

She shook her head. "No, look. I don't even know if it's a problem. If it's a real problem, I mean. It's just I went to the doctor, and the doctor said there was nothing wrong with me. With any of us."

Which to begin with made the doctor a liar, I guessed. After all, there was always something wrong with humans. Delicate mechanisms, humans are. Throw one of them out in the wild and… No, never mind. They thought they went into the wild now and then, and of course some tribes of them lived in the wild. But it made their lives nasty, brutish and short. "So, what's happening, in clear words."

She didn't give it in clear words. To be fair, the problem might have been that she was female and young. Even the female young of my species have trouble getting to the point. She hemmed and hawed around a while, saying she was tired, so tired, which I knew, just from smelling her. Then she said, "But here's the thing. I always wake up more tired than when I go to bed. And so do all my roommates."

"Roommates?"

"I live with four girls, she said. "Rhonda, Anna, Joan, and Mary. I'm Martha, by the way. Martha Robinson."

"Nice to meet you, Martha."

"Yes, well," she tossed her head, sending her shoulder-length hair flying. Humans are lucky they don't have to groom that hair with their tongues. You'd never get dried pigeon blood off that hair. "Thing is, you know, all of us have been having these symptoms. We go to bed and we wake up more tired. And there's nothing we can take or do. We thought it was chronic fatigue syndrome, but the doctors all say there's nothing wrong with us. Of course, they're not very good at discovering what's behind chronic fatigue syndrome, but— Anyway, so we had thought maybe it was something in the house, and we've done all sorts of analysis, but we couldn't detect anything, and then—"

"Yes," I said, interested.

"Well, we moved. And it continued." She made a face. "And Marcy said I should come to see you."

I tapped my tail on the desk. It makes a nice rhythmic sound that helps me think. Okay, fine. It's also the sort of thing cats do when they're annoyed, and this whole thing was annoying. There are things you can't help, okay? They're built in to the back brain. Humans bare their teeth in a peculiar way when they want to show no aggression, and we… well… we do cat things.

I washed my ear while I thought. As Shakespeare's cat would say, that pigeon had a lot of blood in him.

"You know I'm not cheap, right?"

She nodded. "Marcy said a palette of tuna and five hundred dollars."

"That's sort of the minimum," I said. "That's if we solve the case in a day or two. If it takes longer, it will cost you more."

She looked thoughtful but nodded. "We have jobs, all five of us. We'll pay. But only if you find the cause and the tiredness stops."

"All right," I said. "I'll take it."

"Like that?" she said.

"Sure. No guarantees, mind. I don't know what we're dealing with here. If it's something organic, or something of the sort humans should and could discover, it's unlikely I can fix it."

"All right," she said. "You'll want my address."

"No, I'll find you."

She looked suitably impressed. The truth is that human addresses don't make any sense to cats, or even to Protectors.

Look, most human street signs are way above cat level. More importantly, human houses, even for those who can read the numbers, have the numbers way up, over the transom, which makes it really difficult for a cat or, you know, a cat-shaped being to read, unless he's standing across the street.

So, how do we find humans? I'm glad you asked. Thing is, humans leave traces in the environment, long after they cross it, and the places where they live glow with their markings.

Aura is the wrong word, and yet, it might be something very like an aura. I see it as light, anyway, only that I don't see it, precisely, not with my eyes. I sense it would be a better word. Or I see the trail in my mind.

We have reason to think that this too, like the ability to think at humans is something that normal cats had, long before the Protectors came to be. We don't know for a fact, the same way we don't know for a fact that our poor, dumb ancestors could communicate with each other or with humans. We just don't. They couldn't read or write. Not their own script, and not human script either. So, it was, in more ways than one, pre-history for us.

Most Protectors can read and type both human script, at least for their own lands—only a few being polyglots—and also the script we have devised for our own language. When I said earlier that any Protectors reading this would be reading the real report, it is because these records of my cases in human script are for humans only. So now we have communication and history. But before our… uh… *uplifting*, our past is a mystery.

However, I've read paper records of the old days—mostly on my pet's computers, after they've gone to bed—and I know very well that even in the bad old days there were cats and kittens who followed their lost owners halfway across the land. So, I think my poor dumb ancestors could always see those traces in the landscape, of where a particular human had gone. Very useful for tracing our own pets. Who, of course, are quite oblivious. As they are to so many other things.

Martha had got up but hesitated. I twitched my whiskers at her and disposed my mouth as close to a wry human smile as I could. "Go on, toots. I'll catch you up."

She shrugged as though deciding the whole thing was crazy and left. I finished cleaning pigeon blood from my paws. My pets give me canned food, of course, but that pigeon— Never mind. You're human. You're not ready to know why I had to kill the pigeon. Someday, maybe.

I left the office after Martha. I shut the door behind me with a pull of the paw, and then used… well, telekinesis, which you'll sleep better at night if you think I don't have, to lock it. Not that there was anything in there to steal. It was just two old chairs and an old desk. But I'd once left it unlocked and found a human in there who had destroyed his mind with certain type of drugs. These humans can become vessels for invaders, just like the pigeon.

Only humans are much harder to kill.

And we won't even mention how much harder they are to bury. It takes a lot of paws.

Fortunately, there are a lot of Protectors in Goldport. Well, let's be honest, really. There are a lot of Protectors everywhere. In fact, if you are owned by what you think is a cat, or you pass what you think is a feral colony, you'll find they are mostly Protectors. Sometimes half-Protectors.

No, we didn't do it. Actually, humans did it. Look, it takes a certain native intelligence to avoid being neutered. Even then most of us are. But almost every cat who survives out in the wild is a Protector. And it's almost only the Protectors reproducing.

Which should make you wonder where humans got the idea of neutering every pet cat. But it won't. As I said, humans are blind to some things even when they're completely up front and obvious to anyone else.

I left my office via the stairs, a narrow set just outside my door, leading to a non-descript door next to the noisy, student-frequented pizza parlor.

The stairway was dark, with a steep staircase. To my senses, it was crisscrossed with the luminous trails of passing humans, some very faint and months old. Some new and bright. This time there were no threatening, possibly non-human or tainted ones.

The psychiatrist who has the office across from me, the only other office on the second floor—there is a rental office and a marketer on the third—has never caught on that I'm the tenant of M. T. S Confidential Investigations. I'm not exactly surprised.

I still approved of him. Probably in his mid-thirties, with the look of a native of the Indian subcontinent, but a local accent. He looked very tired and sometimes angry at the end of his workday, but always smiled when he saw me, and I rubbed against his legs. He paused long enough to lean down and pet me, and I submitted to it, even letting him pet my moustaches.

He smelled of dogs, but that's all right. We Protectors don't discriminate. And besides, letting him pet me was good for my cover.

Oh, right, okay, fine. So, I actually like getting scratched. It's another of those atavistic things. Most of us do. Some of us even like getting their bellies rubbed, though of course we'd never admit it in polite company and sometimes must scratch the human just to show him his place.

"I guess your owner goes home before you. Very inconsiderate," the psychiatrist said. "You are a good kitten. If you ever need another caretaker, I'm available."

I filed that away as needed. Look, my caretakers are okay, but if they should choose to move, it would seriously mess up my arrangements.

I waited until he'd cleared the stairs, and then walked down after him. Look, it's a thing. I didn't want him looking too closely at me or noting what I was doing. He was a smart man, as far as I could tell, and smart people have a way of noticing things even when they don't want to. There was a good chance he'd figure out I was moving too purposely, as I followed the client's trail. I know people have noticed that about Protectors before. We trot too purposefully. And if it's just a random cat, no one cares that much, but they do notice when it's a cat they know. The other danger is that he'd notice where I went and assume that was the home of my pets. And then try to confront the people there about leaving me alone at the office.

So, I let him get lost in the downtown crowd before I followed the client's trail. Fortunately, she had a clear and well-defined pattern, despite being tired. It's not always the case. I trotted clear past the George, the diner downtown that smelled funny all the time. Someday I'd have to investigate why it smelled funny, and what it meant. But so far, they'd not given me problems, and I was busy. I noted my psychiatrist-friend went in there, which was interesting, as I'd think him more upscale than that.

I trotted on past, turned at the park down the street, and into a street of old Victorians rented out to college students.

There, in an alley between two tall brick buildings was the colony. They are—or at least do-gooders think they are—a feral colony of normal cats living off the scraps of nearby restaurants. They did, in the way of all feral colonies, have some mixes and half-and-halfs. Protector genes seem to be dominant, so most mixes are mostly Protector, but the half-and-halfs are smaller, and sometimes—rarely—mentally slower. But mostly, these were just young Protectors, who had not yet found their calling in life.

Some of them—as I had, when I was much younger—doubted the existence of any real threats to humans, or questioned our mission of protecting humans.

They hung out, ate the easy food, and fought. As I skirted the colony, trying to avoid any confrontations—the young ones were often overly territorial—I heard a fight. Two small, scrawny males were getting into it. It was mostly bluster and shouting, of course. One of them only had half an ear, proof of earlier battles. I'd put my money on him, if I were a betting feline.

I wasn't. I didn't even look at the female they were fighting for, registering her smell of readiness and moving on.

Many young Protectors go wrong and question their mission in life. Some never come back.

I'd not gone more than another quarter block when I heard soft steps behind me and smelled *her*.

Not a ripe smell. Though it wouldn't be long now till her first heat, she was a juvenile. I knew who she was. I half-turned to give her a look over my shoulder and sent the growl-thought at her, "Scram, kid."

She didn't answer in words but sent me back a sense of cheeky amusement. I didn't roll my eyes, because we aren't very well equipped for eye rolling, but I would have if I could. You see, I knew this kid. She was at the juvenile stage where kittens go all gangly and awkward before full maturity. Her fur was medium length, and white. She had startlingly Siamese-blue eyes. Probably descended from the only Siamese-like-Protector-line, in some fraction.

And she was a nuisance.

First, she'd been born at the colony, and had never had a stable home with stable pets who'd look after her. Her hair, which would otherwise be nice and soft, was all dusty and sometimes had debris she'd rolled in. Second, I was the first working Protector she'd met.

Once, months ago, in a good will mission, I'd made the mistake of talking to colony kittens about the noble life of a Protector, and our mission to protect and help the species that had given us sentience. Call it an attempt to snatch brands from the fire. It hadn't worked. I'd talked to about ten of them. I did every spring. But most kittens born in the colony just went on to do what their parents did—mate fast and die young.

All except this one.

She'd caught on to the system of old names—I don't think anyone had ever given her a name, certainly not her parents—and got it all wrong, calling herself Guinevere Bast du Lac. Okay, it was an impressive effort for a colony baby. Where she'd got the names, I didn't know, since I doubted anyone had taught her to read. And she wanted to be a Protector so badly her little tail kinked at the thought.

Only thing is, there's no academy or training program in Goldport. And I had never actually taught a young one. I'd hoped an entire litter would make it to Denver for training, but a little kit? Alone? And a female at that, with her first heat probably starting somewhere on the way?

Plus, born in the colony, with no discipline and no limits? I doubted she'd make it through the academy. Certainly, if she went alone she wouldn't. She'd end up as one of those pathetic little corpses you saw sometimes by the side of a busy highway.

But she had spunk. She continued following me, and after a while said, "Are you on a case, Myth?"

She had a gutter snipe accent, but at least she could project proper words.

"Yes. A dangerous one. Go home, kid."

"Can I help?"

"No. Go home kid." I trotted fasted, winding between people's legs, going past where my client lived, because I wanted to lose her. After a while, it worked, because I stopped hearing anymore of her stupid questions.

After making sure she wasn't around, I traced back to the apartment building, a converted Victorian. There was a door to the apartment on the bottom floor, and another to the stairs leading to the top floor.

Telekinesis works well on locks, if you can master the trick. I got the door open, slipped inside and up the stairs. I could hear many young women talking. I also saw recent traces of four humans, and one very faded one, which was hard to observe.

When I came up the stairs, my client was arguing with her roommates. "I don't care," she was saying. "We have to figure out what's causing this."

"So you hired a cat?" one of them asked, laughing.

I'm not going to bother describing them all. It didn't matter to me, so I don't really remember what they looked like in human terms, and if I describe their traces, it will mean nothing to you. Two of them were brunettes, one was blonde, like Martha, and one was a redhead. The redhead was the only one that interested me, because her traces were weird.

Look, it doesn't mean anything, not normally. Humans have different levels of traces. And some have some kind of a defense that can make them invisible to cats. Deaf to our speaking to them, too. Remember where I said sometimes we had to imitate human words? That's why. Some of them just couldn't hear us. Or chose not to. I never knew if it was one or the other.

But this redhead… well, something felt weird about her. I crouched under a sofa, looking out just enough to observe her. She was the one named Rhonda, and she wasn't as vocal as the others in making fun of Martha for hiring me.

While they sat down and ate, and talked about it, she looked mostly pensive. I wondered if she was actually worried. It's hard to tell, you know?

I found out she worked at a New Age store around the corner, and the only thing she said was there were herbal teas that could solve their problem.

"We've been taking your herbal tea forever, Rhonda," Martha finally said. "It didn't work." She was starting to look mulish. "I know it sounds stupid to hire a cat, but I tell you, he talked in my mind. I could hear him, as if he were human."

I expected Rhonda to say something about the communication with animals, or whatever. I'd met new agers before. They were very useful, in that you could convince them all cats could talk telepathically to humans. Marcy, Martha's friend, was a new ager.

As long as you indulge them about their crystals and stuff they're fine. But Rhonda just frowned.

"Fine, I'll pay his fee myself, if that's what you guys want," Martha said, finally, and went off to her room.

I waited. I waited a long time. I might have dozed. Any good Protector on an investigation masters the fine art of the cat nap, always alert and ready to swing into action.

The "swing into action" part came when I heard a door open, then another, then another. I opened my eyes, and four of the girls, including Martha, were standing there, in pajamas, their eyes glazed. They smelled wrong. They felt wrong.

Rhonda, on the other hand, was fully dressed and smiling. She went to the wall of the apartment, and made some gestures. My fur rose, and it was all I could do not to start yowling a challenge, something I hadn't been in danger of doing by accident since my first month in the Academy.

I knew those hand gestures. More than that, I knew the… for lack of a better word—you humans are really inadequate with words—aura now shining forth from Rhonda. It was strong, and there was something awful about it. Something I'd never seen before.

I sent a warning mentally, knowing it would not reach Denver, but hoping it would be picked up by some watch-Protector between here and Denver and passed on. I'd expected a ghost who was draining the girls of energy. I expected a curse of some sort. I expected anything but this. If I had expected this, damn it, I'd have gotten backup.

*Any Protector, listen and pass on. This is Mithra Tamuras de Shangrila in Goldport Colorado. We have fey. Warning. We have disguised fey. An incursion with harm.*

Chances were, everything was lost already, and no one would hear my warning, and this tear in the human world would go unnoticed, until it would take hundreds of Protectors, most probably losing their lives to fix it.

I should have realized what was going on, you'll say?

In my defense, Rhonda had the best cover-up of any fey I'd ever seen. And she'd been living unnoticed with these people for how long? That wasn't normal for fey. Not normal at all. They're cunning, but usually not that good at disguise.

Besides, when they break in it is usually all about trading and "deals" with the humans, when it's not about kidnapping a nursing woman to nurse their whelps. They're minor league grifters. I had no idea what was going on here, but the waves of power I saw coming through as the cabalistic passes were executed were of such quality that I knew they were opening a portal into fairyland.

Of course, I should have rushed forward and interrupted the passes, and prevented its opening. That is certainly what you're going to say.

But physically, I have the body of a cat, albeit one with some interesting mind-abilities. My heart pounded so hard I could feel it in my ears. All I could think was that if I attacked, then Rhonda—whoever she really was—would tell the other four, for it was obvious they were under her control—to attack me.

And then I would die.

I'd read the odes to Protectors who'd died preventing harm to the human race. I knew I was supposed to lay down my life. But… for nothing?

Light shone forth, blinding. The portal to the other world opened. Through it, I could see what looked like the illustrations of dim and awful Victorian factories, in which many people—in pajamas—labored at a long bench, making something, or packaging something that looked like grey powder in little glass bottles.

Rhonda stood aside and gestured for the four to go through.

Mindlessly, they walked towards the portal.

In my mind, loud as a bell and clear as day, I heard a voice yelling, "For Humans and the Stars."

By the corner of my eye, coming from somewhere behind me, I saw a white fur ball, streaking towards Rhonda.

For a moment, hearing the Protector oath, I'd hoped someone had answered my desperate plea. But now the sudden recognition erupted in loud, mind-talk, "Kid!" Guinevere.

Exactly what I'd said would happen happened. The four sleep-walkers turned to grab at that slip of a girl cat. To my shock, though, Guinevere appeared and disappeared, a flash of a cat now there and now not, claws and fur and then nothing, but gashes still appeared in her wake, as though her claws did damage enough while invisible.

There have been legends. I had no time to ponder it.

From the damage, I assumed Guinevere climbed on Rhonda's head and tore horrible gashes in the elf's flesh, but they healed right away. The four enthralled women tried to join in, but did nothing more than get in each other's way.

I needed iron. And hell and damnation, I hadn't even made a point of wearing a collar with an iron buckle.

I ran like a mad cat. Fortunately, the sleepers had left all their rooms open. I streaked through each one in turn, finding nothing. I had no time to open drawers, damn it.

And then suddenly, in the last room—Martha's—I found a large iron dagger atop some unopened bills. It was ancient and probably some kind of family heirloom.

It was also heavy, and there was no way I could lift it, ever. Not with my body, at least. Sure, I could hold the end between my teeth and drag it. But from the living room came a yowl of pain, and I knew I'd have no time at all.

So I used my mind.

It is one thing to open a lock by telekinesis, and another and quite different to carry a heavy object sixty feet. I don't know how I managed it—desperation, some innate defense mechanism? My mind pushed the dagger, and I ran after it into the living room. There was blood everywhere, and Guinevere was screaming, very loudly.

So, I looked for the right ankle, and pushed the dagger into it, hard.

There was an explosion. Humans were thrown. Rhonda lost all disguise, becoming a shriveled grey monkey-like thing. What elves really are when they are at home.

The portal was closed. On the floor, near where it had been, there was a bundle of fur streaked with blood.

I went to the elf first. Some duties, Protectors can neither shirk nor forget. The elf was not dead, but was close enough as long as that iron dagger stayed in it. And I'd make sure the iron stayed in it.

"Don't touch it, and do not remove the iron," I shouted at the humans, who were looking around and asking questions I had no time for.

I made my way towards the bundle of fur, afraid of what I'd find.

*Mithra Tamuras de Shangrila,* a voice in my mind said. *Your plea has been heard. A team is on the way.*

I didn't even answer back with words. Just an acknowledgement, a mental nod.

I crept on my belly towards the girl cat. I couldn't cry, but I could think of it. All that lovely fur. All that lovely bravery.

Leaning in close, I licked her ear. And realized she was breathing. I rested my head on her neck and purred.

She was the most infernally annoying female I'd ever met or even dreamed of meeting.

There she stood, outside the window of my pets' house. It was a warm night and the window was open, and she sat on the outside while I sat inside. I'd dragged her home with me, that awful day, and the pets, being tender-hearted, had paid for her vet bills. They let her sleep on the porch but were still negotiating on whether to allow her inside.

The word "spayed" had been uttered before I'd managed to think at them what a pity that would be.

So, they let her sleep in the enclosed porch out back. Of course, it made no difference since they let me out. Or I went out. To my office.

But right then I couldn't trust myself outside.

She was the most stubborn collection of fur and meows I'd ever met, and still looked just as beautiful, even though I knew there were scars under the silken fur.

"You will go to Denver," I told her. "Transportation has been arranged. They will teach you what you need to know to be a proper Protector."

"You can teach me what I need to know to be a proper Protector."

Sure, and end up in an early grave, if she pulled more stunts like that one she'd pulled. "No," I said, instead. "I don't have the kinds of powers you have, especially that invisibility thing."

She pouted. It shouldn't be possible for a cat to pout. Or even a Protector. But she pouted. "I don't want to go."

"You have to go," I said. "This thing with the elves… The creature that stayed on this side was interrogated. It turns out they've been kidnapping people all over the world. Giving them small quantities of some hypnotic powder. Then, at night, they take them to the other side, where they control them to make more of the hypnotic powder."

"Why? Why would the elves want so much hypnotic powder?"

"They'll tell you in Denver," I said.

In that moment, a truck stopped in front of the house. The human driving it had no idea why. It had all been arranged.

For a moment Guinevere looked like she was going to resist, but then she pushed her head forward, quickly. Our noses touched through the screen. "Don't go anywhere, Myth," she said. "I'll be coming back."

And then she was gone, a streak of white fur jumping into the back of the truck.

I stayed there, half stretched towards the open window, and gave a deep sigh. In Denver they'd tell her why we shouted "For Humans and the Stars."

There were other worlds and other beings. And our only way to repay our creators was to guard them until they could leave the cradle.

Out there in the universe, bigger dangers than even elves lurked.

But tonight, looking at the stars, I couldn't think of dangers nor of coming fights, but only of a gallant white girl cat, making her way to Denver and training.

She would make a great Protector.

And I'd be here when she returned.

# Where Go the Fae...

**Nathan Throop**

*No, you morons!* Sean O'Donnell mentally shouted. *You can't put a heat sink that far from the reactor. Otherwise there would be no point to having a heat sink. Or passengers, because they'd all die inside a couple hours.*

Sean slashed his stylus at the hologram floating above his desk. The idea that some snot-nosed kid with a brand-new bachelor's degree might try to 'improve' Sean's designs for colony ships made him grind his teeth.

"Dad. Dad! Will you stop making your interns' lives miserable and listen for a minute?" Andrea's voice broke his concentration and brought him back to the conversation.

After taking a moment to remember what they were talking about, Sean said, "Andrea, she's a teenager. The last person in the world she wants to hang out with is her grandpa."

"And that's exactly why she's going to. She needs to get away from those drunk, idiot boys she hangs out with." Andrea's voice was a comfort Sean had not realized he needed and he felt his bad mood start to fade. Even over a video call, she was a force to be reckoned with. Fiery red hair and cold blue eyes—both of which she'd inherited from him—perfectly captured her personality. "It'll be good for you, too. When was the last time you left that run-down trailer you call an office, you hermit? Maybe she'll get you to church, for once."

"Now see here," Sean said, putting on the Dad Voice, "don't you give me lip. I raised you to respect your elders."

"Really? I remember you and Grandpa O'Donnell exchanging a punch or two."

"I said that's how I raised you, not that I was raised that way." It was hard to keep a smile off his face.

Andrea rolled her eyes. "Whatever, old man. I didn't call to ask your permission. I called to tell you that when Cara graduates in four months she's coming to stay with you." She grew quiet and looked away from him. Sean knew his daughter well enough he could see something was bothering her. He also knew unless he wanted his head bitten off, he shouldn't press her to find out what was the matter. A minute passed before she asked what was on her mind.

"You're clearing the land for the Elevator today, right?"

That surprised Sean a little. Andrea hadn't ever asked about the Project before. "Uh, yeah. You know about that?"

She rolled her eyes at him. "It's been all over the news for a few weeks. Hard to miss. Every news feed shows Earth Firsters up in arms. They're alternating between being furious that we're bulldozing one of the world's last wildlife refuges and that we're trying to abandon Earth."

"Is that what you're worried about? Kiddo, the American military is really good at their job. They've managed to keep those nutcases outside the perimeter so well I can't hear their chanting unless I turn on the fence security feeds."

"No, that's not it. I just…" She paused again, then made a disgusted sound before finishing in a rush. "Every time I think about tearing down that Preserve I feel antsy." She waved a hand in a 'get on with it' roll. "You know, nervous…worried. Geez, I'm being stupid."

At that, she dropped the call without even so much as a 'Love you, Dad,' and her holographic image disappeared. This time Sean did laugh at his daughter. She was just like her mother.

But Andrea had a point. When was the last time he'd left his office, or the 'run-down trailer' as she had called it? A glance out the window showed the sky to the east was turning gray, the stars fading. He groaned as he realized he'd spent the entire night in the rusted-out double-wide going over blueprints for the millionth time.

A bladder he had ignored for hours made itself known, and Sean groaned in frustration at his temperamental prostate. There was nothing to do but take care of business, so he rose to his feet. As he straightened he pushed a fist into his lower back, and at the resulting crack he groaned again, this time in pleasure. Age had brought new aches in his bones, but it also brought the intoxicating relief of a joint pop. Sean reflected with a wry smile that he never appreciated relief from pain until he had lived with it on a daily basis.

Instead of heading to the trailer's crusty bathroom, Sean walked out the front door of his office into the cool Irish morning air. He walked around numerous cages stacked up in front of the rusted mobile home, each of which held a wild animal native to Ireland. Squirrels, foxes, owls, even a gray wolf and her cubs, all captured in the Irish Wilderness, waiting to be shipped to a new home. Sean only hoped their new home would be one they could live on.

He'd been on site at the Glenveagh National Park for two months and couldn't get over the primal beauty of the place. With almost every square mile in the world being used for housing, manufacturing, or farmland, there were only a few places left that could truly be called 'wild.' How such a prime piece of real estate as the Park never got developed was a mystery. But Sean was grateful for it for several reasons, not the least of which was that it gave him somewhere other than his office's bathroom to pee.

Two minutes later Sean was feeling much relieved, but his good mood from talking with Andrea faded as he looked at the expanse of trees before him. It was hard not to be sad that in only a few hours they would be razed to make way for the Project.

He stood and admired the landscape trying to remind himself that even if they left it alone, in a hundred years it would still die. But if they could get the Elevator built—if Tau Ceti IV's atmosphere matched the spectroscopy—if they could get Earth plants to grow there, it would all be worth it.

That last thing worried Sean the most. No matter how perfectly designed the Elevator, ships, and habitats were, if they got to Tau Ceti and the plants didn't grow, it would all be for nothing.

As sad as the thought of losing the wilderness made him and as worried as he might be about the future, Sean was also glad to be a central figure behind the Phoenix Project. Twenty-five years earlier, he had experienced a flash of creative insight unlike anything he had ever known since. Over the course of three weeks he'd developed new metal alloys, plans for asteroid miners, and the Space Elevator itself. He felt much like he thought Handel must have when writing *The Messiah*. Thoughts, inspiration, and plans spewed forth from his mind almost faster than he could write. And from them had come the Project.

Sean sighed and turned around to head back to his office and review the plans again.

"Ó Domhnaill, I would speak with you."

At the sound of a woman's voice, Sean spun to face the forest. Standing close to where he'd relieved himself only moments before was a tall woman with deep brown hair. She wore a long brown and green gown, and Sean could see she wasn't wearing shoes. But the thing that most attracted his attention was a black medallion hanging from a leather cord around her neck. It looked like clay and was large enough it might be called an amulet.

"Who are you?" Sean's voice cracked a little from surprise. He cleared his throat and adopted the Dad Voice again. "How did you get in here, young lady?"

"Áine, Lady of the Fae." Her voice was like a sunrise—bright, but distant and cold—and upon hearing it, Sean found it hard to think clearly.

"'Awn-ye?' That's your name?"

The woman, Áine, tilted her head slightly to the side and regarded him for a moment. Her expression reminded Sean of a lion regarding a baby gazelle, trying to decide if eating it would be worth the effort.

"Look, whoever you are, this site is off limits to the public. Later today we're—"

"I know of your intentions for my home. I am troubled that the Lord of Erin would so recklessly intrude on the realm of Fae. Have you forgotten the oaths you swore?" Her voice remained clear and distant, but her eyes bored into Sean's with an intensity that could start fires. The first beams of morning light broke through the trees and Áine's eyes seemed to gather it all to throw back at him, glowing like green embers. "My people are one with the wild. Men have all but killed it, and in so doing have all but killed us."

Sean stifled a groan. Great, she was one of *those*. Some of the Earth Firsters said they were 'Representatives of Gaea,' or some crap like that. Then they called on the powers of nature to simultaneously bring ruin to the Project and save Earth from its fate. In his spare time, Sean liked to review security footage of them being wrestled into police cars.

"Okay, Miss," he held up his hands and walked toward the woman. "I know what the news feeds say about the Project, but we're really not going to destroy the wild. We're going to rebuild it on another planet. Now, it's time for you to go." It only took a few steps to come within reach of the girl and he extended one hand to grab her arm.

Before he could touch the young woman, his hand froze in the air. At first he thought he was having a stroke—the same had happened to his father—and he was sure these would be his last moments on earth. Frost formed on his fingertips. In horror, he watched tendrils of ice reach past his knuckles and up to his elbow.

Sean cried out and fell backward, cradling his frozen hand against his chest. There was no pain except for where warm, pink flesh met blue. As if watching from a distance, Sean reasoned that must mean the arm was dead.

All around him, plants stirred, their leaves rustling and branches creaking. But underneath that sound he thought he could detect laughter. In the shadows of brush and grass there were flashes of multi-colored fur, large eyes, and spindly limbs.

The woman, Áine, didn't move a muscle except to turn her eyes downward to where he lay on the ground.

"The last Man," the way Áine said the word gave it special significance, "who dared touch me was eaten from within by worms. Consider yourself lucky that all I required of you was your arm. I ask again—What of your oaths to the Sidhe?"

Sean started to hyperventilate, unable to tear his eyes away from his arm. "Oaths? What are you talking about? I didn't swear anything! What did you do to my arm?!"

A short exhale of breath and a roll of her eyes were the only reaction Áine gave. "Very well, the oaths your ancestor gave, then. It makes no difference. You are as bound by them as the first Ó Domhnaill was. And I call upon you to fulfill your obligations."

Dimly, in the back of his mind, years of mathematics and logic screamed at him that this conversation couldn't be happening and Áine couldn't be there. The only magic that had ever existed was born of resistors and capacitors, metal stress tables and vector properties, laws of motion and thermodynamics.

His good hand gripped his frozen arm. It felt cold enough to burn his fingers. Almost in self-defense that part of his mind tried to calculate how much heat energy must have been sucked out to freeze it so quickly and thoroughly. Where could that heat have gone? It should have made the air around him boil, but it felt as cool as any summer morning.

Áine's strangely beautiful face twisted into a sneer. "Mortal memories are short, but can you truly remember nothing?" Windblown laughter again drifted out from the surrounding underbrush. "Then listen well, fallen Ó Domhnaill. In recompense for our service sowing the Garden for your mewling first father and mother, we were granted the Isle of Erin as our domain unto the end of the world." She turned away from Sean and walked to the cages that held the preserve's last few captured animals. Her voice softened and seemed to grow wistful. "We crafted it into a garden to rival your lost one, but unlike Men, we knew better than to let any serpent enter our land.

"If only we could have so easily kept Men out." She waved a hand at a cage that held a she-wolf and two cubs, and Sean looked for something to happen. When nothing did, Áine turned back to Sean, her eyebrows drawing down in a frown. "You keep the creatures of nature caged in iron? You truly have left your oaths behind.

"You say you have no memory of your vows? Then I will dredge them from your past." Áine strode to Sean in three quick steps giving him no time to do more than scramble backward on his behind. But she easily caught him by his shirt with one hand, and held her other hand up in a cupping shape. The early morning light swirled as though in a vortex and coalesced into a ball in her outstretched hand. Before Sean could gape at the feat, she slapped it into his face and eyes.

Sean closed his eyes expecting more pain, but instead warmth spread across his face in stark contrast to the cold of his arm. It penetrated into his mind and to Sean it seemed as though parts of his brain he never used were waking up. He opened his eyes again to see the early morning sunlight twist and dance, forming into the shapes of people.

"What did you do to me?" The Dad Voice was gone, replaced by a whisper.

Áine's reply was mild. "I cast the shadows from your mind. Watch and remember."

The image grew sharper until Sean could see it was of a group of people that looked as though they came from one of the badly done fantasy movies his youngest son liked to watch. There was a man, tall and proud with a black beard that reached halfway down his chest and eyes just as dark. He wore leather and linen, and at his waist, a bare bladed sword of dark iron. Blood stained his clothes, giving him an appearance that would have been barbaric if not for the nobility in his eyes and bearing. A man of war satisfied in victory. A severed head dangled from his hand by long hair. With a satisfied look in his eye, the man threw it forward to land upon the ground with a soundless impact. It rolled to a stop in front of another of the figures.

"Nuadha, the Sea People will come to your shores again, bringing their iron and fire. What say you? Have we an accord?" The words appeared in Sean's mind as though echoing out of a cavern.

The other figure—an almost-man in the same way Áine was an almost-woman—had silver hair held back by a leather cord. Around his neck dangled the same black amulet that Áine now wore. He sat on a chair made of twisting branches, mushrooms, and grass.

"Niall, we thank you for the aid your people have rendered, but we have no need of it. If these Men return to battle, we will drive them back. And if they yet come, we will ensure they cannot again." With that, the silver-haired being touched the swirling black amulet.

The black-bearded man, Niall, bowed his head and with clear respect in his voice said, "Lord of the Fae, your magics are powerful, but neither they nor your bronze can withstand iron. When these men come again, they will set this land to fire so it burns for a century. Smoke will shroud the skies and your people will die."

The light-phantom of Nuadha sat motionless in his throne for long seconds, his head cocked to the side and his eyes staring at nothing. Then in a smooth motion that was reminiscent of a cat entering a bright room, the Fae King stood and looked down regarding the head that lay at his feet.

"Listen closely, Man, to the King of the First Race." Nuadha spoke softly, but the words rebounded within Sean's mind. "If these Sea People come. If the land falls. If my people die with it, then the race of Men will not long survive us. Hear the pronouncement I make in this the seat of my power: Where go the Fae, so go Men. On the day Nature is killed and my people pass into the void, Men will follow." He grasped the black amulet in his right hand so tightly that the edges must have cut him. When he opened his hand again, he held it over the head on the ground and blood dripped from deep wounds in his palm and fingers. "This I vow."

At the last word, a wave of…something—Sean couldn't be sure what, only that it held power—burst out of the amulet at Nuadha's neck rocking everyone at the meeting backward a step. It was then that Sean saw Áine was among the crowd of onlookers.

The tall man was the first of all present to recover himself. He spoke, anger present in both his words and bearing. "King Nuadha, did you make no provision for my people? If you perish, are we to share the fate of those who killed you?"

The king made no answer but to close his fist, cutting off the flow of blood onto the severed head.

With a roar, Niall ripped the sword from his belt and flung it spinning through the air to bury itself hilt deep into the throne, missing the Fae King by inches. Then he strode forward to grab Nuadha by his slight shoulders, so they were face to face.

"How often have we stood by you?! How often have we shed blood and sweat side by side in battle? How often would we have defended you and yours with our lives? Faithless fairy!"

A smile that was neither amused nor pleased creased Nuadha's face. The expression a wolf showed before a meal. "Lord Niall, I know of your valor, and more importantly, I know of your love for your family. The truth of your words rang in my ears: If the Fae are to survive the advent of iron, we will need Men for allies."

"So you thought to force what we would have given freely?"

"The lives of Men are short and what shouldn't be forgotten is all too often left by the wayside. How long before we would have again stood alone? How long would you and your heirs face the bloody waves? How long before my people are cast from this land? A generation? Two?"

Niall growled deep in his throat, violent nature showing through his civilized veneer. His fingers tightened on the Fae King's shoulders to the point that Sean was sure at any moment the crack of broken bones would sound.

But then nobility returned to Niall's features and he straightened, letting go of Nuadha's shoulders. Without a word, one of the man's hands enclosed the black amulet and with a jerk ripped it downward breaking the leather cord. The King didn't respond except to tilt his head.

Niall turned to stand over the bloody head still laying on the ground. The fist with the amulet raised in imitation of what the Fae King had done moments before. Niall tightened his hand and again blood began to drip.

"As you have bound Men to you, Lord Nuadha, so do I bind you to me. This I swear: So long as I and my line live we will preserve the lives of the Sidhe and ensure you have a home. Only give me strength and insight to fulfill this oath and it will be so."

With the last word, Niall threw the twice-blooded amulet to land at Nuadha's feet.

The King looked down at it, then his gaze lifted to regard Niall. "It will be so."

At those words, another wave of force lanced out to strike Niall. The man arched his spine throwing his head back, and although he appeared to be in pain, no sound escaped his lips but the grinding of teeth. Cords stood out on Niall's neck and his fists clenched squeezing more blood from the injured hand.

"As you demand, you and your heirs will understand how to protect my people and have the strength to do so. And should you fail, the doom I pronounced will fall."

When Niall sat up, Sean could see his hair had changed from black to red as deep as any rose and his eye shone blue as a summer sky. Sean gasped as he saw the colors that greeted him every time he looked in the mirror.

The vision faded and the light from which it had been formed returned to its natural configuration. Áine released Sean's shirt and removed her hand from his head.

Sean's first thought was to reject what he'd just seen. After all, there were at least a dozen ways the scene with Niall and Nuadha could have been generated. But even as he opened his mouth, certainty descended. Those hadn't been images. They were memories. Not his memories, but they were in his mind all the same.

"Do you know your duty, Man?" The way Áine said 'Man' made it sound like an insult. "My people walk the edge of extinction and wait for your hand to save us. Do you know the fate of Men should you fail?"

"This…this is insane." Sean wanted to believe he was dreaming, or failing that, that he had actually lost his mind. He mused that long hours arguing with engineers and oversight committees might have that effect on a person. But deep down, just as he knew the vision was not fantasy, but rather memory, he also knew what the fairy woman said was true.

Áine nodded once. "Madness it may be, but it is no less true. Save my people, or yours die."

Sean's voice took on a note of desperation, "Listen to me. Thirty years ago a nomad planet passed through the solar system. It came close enough to Earth to throw off our orbit—you had to have seen it in the sky—and in another hundred years this planet will be dead!"

"You try to blame your inaction, your cowardice, on something you saw in the sky? It is of no import. I can turn a lifeless rock into a garden to rival the first Garden. And with it, my kin will live again."

"You don't understand! The U.N. has already approved clearing the land for the Space Elevator. The last twenty-five years of my life have been building up to this. In three months' time, a cable a hundred meters thick will be lowered from orbit to land right here. We have to get the site ready. The bulldozers are arriving today, for heaven's sake!"

Áine scoffed. "Is this the line of the Ó Domhnaill? My father blessed you with strength and insight to overcome any force, and you balk at this…UN? They are no match for the arts of the Fae."

Under his breath Sean mumbled, "You've obviously never dealt with a bureaucracy."

But despite his own doubts, Sean's mind began to spin through a myriad of options. The flurry of thoughts flying through his brain as they had when he'd devised and designed the Space Elevator. In bare moments, he accepted some ideas and rejected others, instantly knowing which had merit and which had no chance of working.

"We have been patient and forgiving as Men have spread over the earth, encasing it in iron and," Áine's lips twisted, "electricity. Though it killed my father, we watched for centuries as Men spread their influence and ours diminished. No longer. Tell me, shade of the Ó Domhnaill, how will you save my people and yours?"

And in that moment, he knew what he had to do.

Sean let his shoulders slump, as if in defeat, and said, "Well, my Lady, if we're going to save your land, I suppose we should let the animals go."

The only expression that crossed Áine's face was a smirk of triumph. She nodded and stepped back to allow him access to the cages.

With a groan, Sean rose to his feet cradling his frozen arm to his chest and walked to the largest cage, the one Áine had tried to open with the wolves inside. He pressed a thumb to the scanner causing the door to swing open.

The she-wolf within snarled and leaped forward, her teeth bared, ready to rip Sean's throat. With a shout, he fell back holding up his frozen arm to ward off the huge predator. The wolf grabbed hold of the dead limb and began to thrash back and forth, tossing Sean like a doll.

"My Lady," Sean shouted, "help me! I can't save you if I'm dead!"

Even over the snarling of the wolf trying to kill him, Sean heard the Fae Lady sigh in exasperation. Then she strode forward, her hand held forward toward the wolf with a ball of light in her grasp. The animal whimpered and shrank back into the cage where her cubs waited, and Áine stood between Sean and the cage.

"Truly, set against your forebears you are nothing. Any hope I had—"

Her words were cut off as Sean placed a foot on her backside and launched her forward. With a squawk, she flew into the cage and bounced off the rubberized iron mesh on the other side. Then

Sean scrambled to the cage door and swung it shut just as the wolf leapt at him again. The door closed with a soft beep.

Áine picked herself up and looked around, disorientation clear on her face. Then her eyes widened when she saw she was surrounded by iron. From the tree line came hateful murmurs and Sean spun expecting to be attacked. But whatever things made the sounds remained out of sight.

The Sidhe Lady screamed at him through the rubber coated bars of the cage, and the wolf at her side snarled in echo. "Release me! Release me or you will have rejected your duty and I will unleash the plague!"

"No. I won't let you out." Sean was amazed at how calm he sounded.

With another scream—half rage, half triumph—Áine ripped the black amulet from her neck and held it in both hands. "Then you will be the first of Men to die."

The muscles in Áine's arms tightened as she applied force to the amulet. It did not break—didn't so much as chip. The Fae Lady's eyes flicked to Sean and then back to the amulet. With a grunt she strained again to break the clay ornament, but again it held.

She threw her head back and called to the sky. "Father! Why have you allowed this to come to pass?"

Sean eyed the surrounding bushes, wary that something out of a fairy tale might emerge. But then the sound of approaching engines reached his ears, and the undergrowth rustled with retreating footsteps.

Sean sighed in relief, then turned to Áine. "Your father charged my ancestor to save you, not to obey your orders. As long as I work to protect you and yours, you can't unleash your plague. And you know what? Your father's blessing told me how to save you, but you're not going to like it."

"Grandpa, how do you know this is going to work? My biology teacher says even if we are able to get to another world, the plants and animals we send probably won't be able to grow there. He says we shouldn't waste our time and money trying to make another Earth."

All around the room, engineers and astrophysicists glanced at her with annoyed expressions on their faces. They had heard similar comments for years and it was clear they didn't want to hear them again at the Elevator launch party.

"Cara, you graduated high school two weeks ago. You know what that means?"

The question seemed to throw her, because the look she gave him was even more disgusted than her usual expression. Cara shook her head.

"It means," Sean said with a wink, "that you don't have to listen to that idiot anymore."

Sean looked at the feed showing the interior of the first climber filled with plant and animal life. The feed was fixed on a group of iron cages that to most people looked empty. But to his eye they were filled with creatures out of fairy tales, and in the largest, most comfortable cage sat a woman with soil-dark hair and green eyes. Those eyes were fixed on the camera feed and Sean imagined she was looking at him. The look she gave made Sean glad she was heading to another planet and that he was too old to follow.

The thought occurred to him that where the Fae once had bound Men to serve their purpose, now Men returned the favor.

He turned to look out the window, smiled at the ascending climber, and hugged Cara to his side with his remaining arm. "Sweetheart, your biology teacher might be a pretty smart guy, but he has no idea how nature really works."

"What?" Cara asked, confusion plain on her face. She wiggled to get out of Sean's sideways hug, but he didn't let it bother him.

"Nature is magic. We can define biochemical pathways, observe gradients and reactions, and categorize organisms all we want. But when we get down to it, we don't know how life came to be, and I don't think we'll ever learn using the tools we have now. There are laws of the universe that science doesn't even conceive yet. Laws that can't be understood unless we use faith."

Cara's confused expression faded, and she rolled her eyes. Grandpa O'Donnell was talking about supernatural crap again, an obvious sign of the senility the whole family was sure he suffered from.

Sean laughed at her teenager-ness. It was natural that she didn't believe him, but with her dark red hair and sky-blue eyes, someday it would fall to her to deal with Áine and the Fae. So if she needed something to shake her out of her disbelief, he could give it.

The memories unlocked by Áine weren't limited to the bond's creation, and Sean had learned many things. A quick glance around the room showed that no one paid Sean and Cara any mind.

Reaching out his remaining hand, Sean grabbed a nearby beam of early morning sunlight and squeezed it into a ball. Cara gasped loudly, but before she could say anything Sean put a finger to his lips to tell her to be quiet. Fortunately, she obeyed.

Sean grinned at his granddaughter, then threw the sunlight ball so that it struck her in the face. A splash of light spread over Cara's face and across her eyes. Then an instant later it dissipated and the sunbeam returned to its proper place in the room.

This time, Cara did cry out and every face in the room turned to look at them. Sean laughed nervously and said the first thing that came to mind, "It's okay. She just tried her first jalapeno."

Before she could say anything, Sean took hold of Cara's elbow and led her away to a remote corner of the room. She hissed at him, "Grandpa, what was that?!"

"That was a splash of sunlight to banish shadows from your eyes." Sean held out a pad to her. "Cara, this is a feed of the crawler's interior. Take a look."

"You've shown me the crawler's interior a hundred—"

"Take another look."

Cara growled but still did as she was told. Sean knew what she would see. The crawler was filled with hundreds of cases and cages holding plant and animal life. But all around them, huddled into corners, were creatures that until that moment she had never seen anywhere but on a movie screen. Some were furry, some had dragonfly wings, some had pig snouts. And in the center, still in an iron and rubber cage that she shared with a wolf and cubs, sat Áine.

"Grandpa, who is that?" Cara sounded as stunned as he had been the first time he'd seen the Fae Lady.

Sean turned to look out the window at the crawler as it ascended the massive cable that stretched up into space.

"Sweetheart, there is so much for you to remember, and I'll help you every step of the way. But for now, there is just one thing you need to understand."

The crawler that held what was left of the Sidhe passed out of sight as it entered Ireland's perpetual cloud cover. It and the Fae Lady within were on the way to the transport ships and then to Tau Ceti IV.

"'Where go the Fae, so go Men.'"

# Gamble

Lehua Parker

Under the hazy glow of a streetlight, Tyche taps her stiletto heel, careful to keep her sequined dress clear of alleyway grime. We're a long way from Fifth Avenue, but Tyche always looks like she stepped out of a high-class department store window or salon.

Me, not so much.

A hand on her hip, she says, "Jace, honey, it ain't complicated. You hold the dice. You think of the girl—"

"—Lydia," I say. "Her name is Lydia."

"Yeah, whatever. You think of Lydia. You shake the dice twice for luck, pucker your lips and blow 'em a kiss, then chuck 'em nice and easy. The roll tells you all you need to know."

"That's it?"

"That's it."

Above us, light shines through the curtains of the second story window in a brownstone apartment. I can just make out the curve of Lydia's body propped unnaturally in a chair and the shapes of the skin-suited Idylwyrn thugs hovering around her. There's no sign of Harlan Fairfox of the Unseelie Court, but once the Feywild portal opens, all bets are off.

I can't lose Lydia again.

I can't.

Standing in the shadows below the fire escape, Tyche slips the dice into my palm and says, "You'll rescue the girl—or not. That's up to you. But hurry. My dice and I are headed to Monte Carlo to fleece a whale."

I hold the dice up to the light. They don't look like much, just two six-sided cubes, each side numbered one through six; the wood so old, the edges and corners are rounded. I rub my thumb along dots burned black and deep. Against my skin, the dice are smooth, warm—

*Alive.*

I swallow.

Tyche tousles and primps her hair, fluffing and smoothing perfection. For a moment, the scent of jasmine and winter musk covers the smell of cat piss and fried onions.

"C'mon," she says, flapping a hand at me. "Shake 'em like you mean it. Tick-tock, big guy. I ain't got all night. Neither do you."

"I thought they'd be different," I say, tilting them this way and that. "I dunno, Ty. They remind me of Cracker Jack prizes. Where's my baseball card and Bazooka gum? Where's the comic strip with the corny joke?"

"Seriously, Jace?"

"Don't get mad. I'm just surprised that your famous dice are just shoddy chunks of wood marked with charcoal. Why not ivory or gold or—"

"Or what, genius? Diamonds and jade? Because valuable things only come in shiny packages, right?"

She gives me the once over, drinking in my too-long legs, sleeveless hoodie, and fire-licked face.

I try not to flinch.

"All I'm saying is I expected something else. Something substantial," I say.

Her eyes narrow.

"My dice are carved from a branch of the Tree of the Knowledge of Good and Evil, you moron. Of course they're wood," she says. "Of course they're worn. They're older than—"

"What? Dirt? Dirt's nothing, Ty. Dirt's yesterday. Now if you'd said older than time—now that's old. And, I gotta say, a little cliché, even for you."

She rolls her eyes.

"Puh-leeze," she says, reaching into her evening bag for a pack of Virginia Slims. She shakes out a cigarette and lights up.

Tyche smokes when she's pissed. Pissed is good. Pissed is off-balanced and right where I want her.

She drops her lighter and snaps the bag shut.

"Those dice are plenty valuable, Jacie. Trust me," she says, pulling smoke deep into her lungs.

"I do, Ty. I trust you and your word more than you know."

Wiggling my fingers, I watch the dice dance.

It's the biggest gamble of my life.

Tyche bites back a sigh.

"Stop gloating," she says. "It's annoying."

"I'm not gloating."

"You won, okay? Do you need to hear it? Fine. Jace won. A mortal beat me. There. I said it. I don't know how, but you did."

"I won because you think losing is an option. It isn't. I did what I had to do to beat you, Ty. I'll do anything to save Lydia."

I give the dice a quick shake in my palm, then hold them tight as I brush my knuckles against my lips.

I say, "With these dice, I can't lose. I know it."

She grins like Erinyes, curdling the blood in my veins.

"You think because you roll them, you're guaranteed the result you desire? You flatter me," she says and bobs her head. "That takes way more mojo-juice than I've got. The dice don't let you choose, you know. They don't influence destiny. They just reveal it."

The tip of her cigarette glows as smoke wafts toward me.

Menthol.

I hate menthol. It's fake. Chew gum or smoke, people. You're not fooling anyone.

Wrinkling my nose and fanning my face, I say, "Seven is six and one, two and five, three and four. Those are good odds. Much better than one and one."

Tyche closes her eyes and inhales until a long line of cigarette ash crumples and falls.

I've pushed her to her limits, but she opens her eyes and answers me civilly enough.

"Mortal odds have nothing to do with it. With these dice, there are only two options. Roll a seven, and you'll know bursting through the door will rescue the girl. Rolling snake eyes means—"

"I die if I try. Yeah, you've made that clear."

She sticks out the tip of her tongue. With nails the color of oysters, she daintily picks a speck of tobacco and flicks it into the darkness.

"So do it already," she says. "Chop-chop."

I shake my head. "There's no need. Regardless of the dice, I'm going in. I won't let Harlan Fairfox or his cronies take Lydia through the portal."

"Seems to me, knowing if you're going to die if you attack now would lead a person—a *smart* person—to make a different choice."

I shrug.

"You looking for a cherry on top? Fine. Here you go: more time doesn't change destiny or fate, Jace—they're inevitable. Roll 'em. You'll see."

"Stop rushing me. I won my roll fair and square," I say.

She closes her eyes and blows smoke through her nostrils like a yogi searching for peace.

"Yes," she says "You did. Every being Seen and Unseen knows I pay my gambling debts, Jace. You want to know if you'll rescue the girl? Toss the dice. I don't care either way."

Another deep drag takes the burn down to the filter. By the nicotine stains on her fingertips, the Goddess of Chance loves her smokes. Maybe goddesses don't worry about cancer or taxes or death.

She reaches into her bag again, this time conjuring lipstick the color of pomegranate blood. She smirks as she tints her lips.

"Tell you what, Jacie. If you roll snake eyes, I'll take you to Monte Carlo. You'll get a kick out of my whale—arms dealer, prostitution, child trafficking—there's something special about winning evil money."

I think about the kidnapped woman in the apartment above and what will happen to her—to us—if I don't succeed.

It's not a happy thought.

Tyche purses her lips, then lights another cigarette.

Feigning boredom, she blows a smoke ring.

"Fish or cut bait, Jace."

I clench my hand into a fist, squeezing the dice tight.

"No."

"No? What do you mean, no?"

She flicks ash at me.

"Roll. The. Damn. Dice. Jace. That's the whole point of winning them. You're being ridiculous."

I shake my head, lift the leather lace from around my neck, and pull my medicine bag out. Without looking, I open it and dump in the dice, letting them rattle and come to rest next to a four-leaf clover and a dried mole's ear. Pulling the strings tight, I tuck the bag back under my hoodie.

"You bet me a roll of your dice, Tyche, but you didn't say when I had to do it."

Tyche's ennui vanishes in a heartbeat.

"You wouldn't dare!" she says.

It's my turn to grin.

"Oh, I dare, Ty. I'm risking it all on the fact that if I enter the apartment with your dice and lose, you'll lose even bigger."

"Give me back my dice!"

"When I'm done. That's the deal."

"Oh, you're done, Jace. You're so done."

Talons sprout from fingernails, teeth lengthen, wings erupt from shoulder blades. Her voice growls with all the hate and heat of Hades.

"Roll my dice now, or I'll feed your liver to Cerberus. The Furies will knit stockings from your entrails."

I wag a finger at her. "Not so fast. A bet's a bet, right? The dice are mine until I roll."

She snaps the cigarette at my face.

I lean to the left.

The cigarette passes harmlessly over my shoulder.

I've had flames flung at me before—my scars prove it. A lit cigarette is nothing.

She should know better.

I beat her once before, didn't I?

Deep breath.

"Tyche, I need you to listen. I'm not wasting my roll on something I already know: this *is* the time to rescue Lydia. If they take her through the portal, she's gone forever. Every minute she spends in Feywild is a year or more here. Losing is not an option. So, if you ever want your precious dice back, it's not just me who's going against Harlan Fairfox, it's *we*."

Her wings unfurl.

Car alarms go off.

Our eyes lock. We both know whomever blinks first, loses.

"You sure you want to play, little man?" she says. "These stakes are way out of your league. Last chance. Roll or I'll take them from you."

"You can't."

"Watch."

"To be clear then, by taking back the dice before I roll, you acknowledge that the great goddess Tyche is *welshing* on our bet?"

I'm all in.

She stands there, blinking, a fireball in one hand, her beaded Gucci bag in the other.

I go for the throat.

"Of course, it doesn't have to be just you and me against Harlan Fairfox, Ty. I'm sure you've plenty of powerful friends to invite to our rescue party. The more the merrier—and the more likely you'll get your dice back."

I quirk my eyebrow and smile.

It takes her only a second that feels like an eternity to snuff out the fireball and fold back her wings.

"Fine!" she hisses. "I'll call in my markers. But when this is over, it's still not over."

Raising her head to the moon and howling a curse, she vanishes, leaving only the afterglow of a rude gesture to scorch the hair off my arms.

Guess luck's not such a lady after all.

In the apartment above, I hear voices as more lights flick on. Tyche and her reinforcements better be quick. I touch the dice through the medicine bag around my neck and stare at the window.

Lydia, I'm coming.

Losing is not an option.

# If the Shoe Fits

Rafael Hohmann

Sand-blasted wind, hot enough to cook a biscuit, stroked the back of Harold's liver-spotted neck. He snorted and hacked, which led him into a fit of coughing. Heaven's almighty, felt like he would bark out his ol' lungs on the sand. Sounded like a mare stuck in the mire. Hel'ov'a'sound. He'd had a one-eyed cat twenty-some years make the same noise every night, always leaving behind a wet wad of hair for him to step on in the morning. Dumb thing had thrown itself off their fifth-floor apartment balcony chasing a magpie. Laurane had sworn it was some pixie-whatsit, but that woman was always swearing racoons in the bins were homeless gnomes collecting tin to trade for coins, pipes a'clacking in the walls were brownies fixin' the city sewer system, and so on.

"Manners," Laurane quipped next to him. His wife held herself up straight with her hands together against her chest. She only ever maintained that posture when she was really excited. If she was eager about somethin', that meant Harold would have no chance of changing her mind about it. Her frail frame was not bothered by the occasional blast of wind. She didn't look sweaty or hot like he did out in the smack-dab middle of desert nowhere, New Mexico. For all he knew, she was enjoying the temperature. Always cold, that woman.

"That's one big boot," he muttered, putting an edge to his voice that was meant to tell his wife he was not accepting of this idea. "A boot. Not a house. In the middle of nothin'. No water. No TV."

"It has a door, doesn't it?" Laurane replied. "And such a nice shade of yellow! Two little windows on either side…Oh my, look, I didn't notice it before, but there's a little sitting spot on the instep! You can drink your lemonade and watch the sunset Harold. Won't that be nice?"

"It's a boot," Harold repeated. "Big as a house, but it ain't no house."

Now Harold had been around the block. He was no green reed. He knew there were men out there in the world who preyed on the older folk, tricking them into risky investments, enticing them out of their retirement funds. It was 1969. The world had gotten too smart for its own good. There were men out there who didn't mind robbing from the elderly. If it involved money, morals were out of the question. Two times. Two times he had caught Laurane on their house phone near gift-wrapping their bank account information to send to some fae-king living in Nairobi who had hand-picked them to inherit his fortune of rubies and leprechaun gold. All this nonsense with fairies. His wife believed they existed like a cowboy believes Texas to be the heart of the West—which it was.

Laurane pushed and picked at her dark-blue velvet dress and felt at her silver hair to check if any strands had escaped her bun. "A real dwarf, Harold! I won that sweepstake and we get to meet a real dwarf, and he's going to give us a house!"

"That ain't right, Laurane. You can't go 'round calling people with dwarfism names like that. All folks are the same, just like you and I, no matter how they look. And this is some sort of trick. Beguiling elders into the desert to rob them, is what this is!"

"He's no human, Harold! He's a real dwarf!" his wife replied. She did not comment on his qualms against driving so far from civilization, nor the potential danger they could be facing. She had gotten really good at ignoring his frustrated retorts.

The door to the massive boot opened and a little figure emerged. Laurane gasped in joy. "Here we go." Harold sighed.

It was a broad man, fully dressed in a bright periwinkle-blue three-piece suit tightly-fit to his strong frame. He had a cocoa-colored beard down to his chest, a brow that came out and down far enough to half-cover his eyes, and a fat, curved nose. And he was small. Two, maybe three feet tall. Two rows of perfectly white teeth greeted them in a smile as the man hurried forward with a quick step. "Now that's a pretty sight there, it is! A couple forged together through time and love, supporting each other in their moment of celebration! Brings a tear of joy to my eye, it does!"

"Forged together through sheer stupidity," Harold muttered under his breath. No one heard him.

The realtor had a drawl to the way he spoke, which Harold had to admit was becoming of him, but that meant little. He was still in the middle of the desert standing in front of a boot the size of a barn.

"I—I'm Laurane," his wife stuttered. "And this is my husband Harold. Harold, shake the man's hand!"

Harold scowled, and made sure everyone saw he had—but he shook the man's hand anyway. The realtor's grip was strong and firm, professional.

"I'm Jim," the small man stated with a bow. "And let me tell you Laurane—Harold—you both are as lucky as a pastor collecting tithes from a congregation full of lottery winners! This here is the Horizon Estate, hand-crafted from the finest Peruvian leather, the foundational sole thick and stable, and with not two, but three floors!"

"I hate stairs. My knees can't handle them," Harold growled. Jim and Laurane either did not hear him or had chosen to ignore him.

"And get this," Jim continued, "a hundred acres of property! All around you, everywhere you can see, that's all yours! A better prize you could not find! Congratulations on winning the Amarillo Lucky Pixie Sweepstakes!"

"Oh, sweet mercy!" Laurane squealed. "We've been blessed, we've been blessed! The king of the Fae Folk heard my prayers and accepted me as a believer! I knew the good people would recognize me some day!"

"Laurane," Harold groaned, embarrassment burning his cheeks, "now don't be saying stuff like that." Jim did not seem to mind at all. Instead, the realtor's smile widened. "Indeed, pretty miss, indeed."

"Don't you encourage her, you!" Harold barked, wagging a finger at Jim. "I may be a well-done steak, but I can knock out teeth with the best of them! Fairies don't exist, and this here is a sham! If you push this trick, you'll get what's comin' to you!"

Jim stepped back and bowed, face showing hurt.

"Harold!" Laurane gasped. "You take that back and apologize now!"

Jim held out his hands, palms-up in peace. "I understand, Laurane. It's alright. I've taken no offence, I haven't. How would anyone expect to believe in us in this day and age? Can you believe they have these machines now showing up in businesses and them fancy universities that can calculate math and logistics? Computers. Crazy world. Humans are inventing their own magic."

"There's no such thing as magic. Me and the missus are out of here," Harold snapped, fishing in his pocket for his car keys.

Jim got a gleam to his eyes. It was a look that Harold did not like one bit. "If I can show you real magic. Three real magic actions, will you believe me and admit we exist?"

"Yes, yes, yes!" Laurane gasped giddily. "Real magic! Say yes, Harold! Please, oh please!"

Harold chuckled. "Jim, I can spot a con from a mile away. I've been to Vegas and I've gone backstage to talk to them real professional magicians. I know the tricks. Go ahead, if you can convince me fairies are real, *I promise to accept the boot as a house*."

Jim held up a finger. "Making promises to the Fae Folk holds more meaning than you might think. Alright, let us begin." Jim rubbed his hands together and cracked his knuckles. "Harold, this is to convince you, so you tell me what kind of magic you want to see."

"Turn the land into cotton-candy."

Jim spread out his arms and snorted. "I'm not a Pagan God, Harold. Just a standard dwarf with some borrowed spark."

"Make a glass of fresh raspberry lemonade appear in my hand then."

Jim shrugged and gave a wry smirk. "Already done."

Harold nearly jumped out of his shoes and popped both of his arthritic knees in the process. In his right hand was a crystal glass full to the brim with raspberry lemonade! Some splashed over his arm and his shirt as he sloshed the contents back and forth. Ice cubes clacked with an enticing sound. The glass was real—cold to the touch. "How'd you…in my hand…never felt it…" Harold spluttered.

"Drink it," Jim offered. "I bet it's good."

Laurane was clapping wildly, nearly in tears. Harold looked around, trying to spot Jim's assistant. There had to have been someone else out there with them. Someone who had snuck the glass into his hand while he was distracted. He could not see anyone. The desert was flat and empty, with only a distant set of hills to break the horizon. He hesitantly took a sip of the lemonade. *It was good.* Cold and fresh, a tart zing blended with the sweet of the raspberries. It went down good too, cooling his throat. Harold had not realized just how dry his mouth had been.

"I can't have read your mind, Harold," Jim stated. "No way I could have prepared in advance of you coming here, knowing you would have asked for such a thing. *Magic.*"

Harold shook his head. "Sleight of hand. You won't fool my senses again. See this here wedding ring?" Harold held up his hand. "Hasn't come off my finger in over forty years. Gold's all faded dull. You turn this ring from gold to sparkling silver. I'm watching it. Not even blinkin'. Go right ahead."

Jim smirked. "Harold, my friend—"

"I'm not your friend," Harold snapped.

"Harold, watch closely. I will do as you have asked."

"Snake-tongued liar." Harold chuckled. He focused on the ring and refused to blink, waiting for a change. With no warning, it did. From gold to silver, the transition of color so quick he thought he had imagined it.

"Strap me to a saddle and send me into the ocean…" Harold gasped.

Laurane was practically jumping up and down as she shouted, "Magic is real! Real!"

"Last request? Something to really convince you?"

Harold was shaking his head. It couldn't be… His wife could not have been right all those years… That cat of his that had jumped off their balcony, it couldn't have been chasing after a pixie… "Clone me."

"Clone you?" Jim asked with a frown.

"Yeah, clone me. Like they do to people on them sciency space shows kids like to watch on those new colored TVs."

Jim looked to Laurane. "Are you good with this?"

At first Harold's wife was silent, her mouth open. Then she promptly closed it and shrugged. "If you clone him enough times, maybe there will be a version of him that picks up after himself and helps with the dishes."

Jim nodded. "Harold, your final request—will it convince you if I do this? It will cost me the last of my spark."

Harold nodded solemnly. "If you clone me, come rain or drought, come the angels out of heaven itself, I swear I'll believe you. Otherwise you can kiss my spurs and walk on out'a here."

"Walk straight on out," Second Harold agreed.

"Yep," Third Harold added.

Real Harold shrieked and fell on his rear, dropping the last of his lemonade. To his right and left were two copies of himself! Both of them were frowning and surly-looking, with weathered, gnarled arms folded over their chests. Both of them wore the same tan buttoned shirt and church pants.

"I never saw no magic," Second Harold complained. "I'm not believing anything!"

"You dropped the lemonade," Third Harold complained. "I'm thirsty."

Laurane walked around them in a circle, eyes wide as she examined them from every angle. "It's uncanny, Jim! They look perfectly identical down to the last hair!"

Harold stood back up, swearing and wiping the dust off of himself. His heart couldn't take this sort of shock. Third Harold examined his hand. "Hey, who switched out my wedding band for this silver ring?"

"Your promise?" Jim urged.

"I…I believe," Real Harold replied, dumbfounded at the words coming out of his own mouth. "I believe in fairies."

Laurane rushed forward, moving faster than she had ever done in her old age, and embraced him. "Finally, you old fart! Oops, I hope I'm hugging the right one of you!"

"You never hug me like that," Second Harold complained.

"How do I get rid of these other two?" Harold asked. "I don't want them permanently."

Jim shrugged. "I need to go haggle for more spark. I got nothing left now. You'll have to deal with them."

"Dumb goblin! I don't want these two following me around!"

"Dwarf," Jim corrected dryly. "And you were the one who asked for them. Now they're your responsibility. Feed them and house them."

"My apartment only has one bedroom," Harold spat. "I can't house two more!"

Jim beamed and motioned to the massive boot behind him. "Sir, you and the missus won this place, you did! Why would you ever worry about an ol' crummy apartment again?" Jim tossed him a set of keys. Harold caught them.

"That's the keys. Go check it out! Just step inside!"

"Gimme those," Second Harold said, snatching them from Real Harold.

"I'm the man, I get them." Third Harold argued.

"You pig-kisser, all three of us are men!" Harold snapped, grabbing the keys back and marching to the massive boot-house. The other two Harolds and Laurane followed. Harold fit the key into the lock, a big iron one with fancy carvings around it, and opened the door.

"Fwew, smells like a boot," Second Harold complained.

"Let it air out," Jim called out. "It's brand new, so the wall paint is still drying."

Harold and his gaggle stepped inside and into the shade. "This ain't no house!" Third Harold cried out.

"It's a huge room! No stairs, no hallways, no kitchen, no nothing!" Real Harold shouted. "It's just the inside of a boot!"

"Where's all the furniture?" Laurane asked with a frown.

The door to the house closed behind them, and the sound of a bolt sliding over the frame followed. Jim's voice called back from the other side, "It's a modern design! You can add rooms as you like!"

"You said there would be three floors!" Harold shouted. "I knew it! It's a con! Let us out of here!"

Harold pounded on the door, but it held fast. There was no way out. The inside of the boot looked exactly as one would imagine it would, bland and empty. To one end a beam of sunlight shone down, where the opening to the top of the boot was. "No way I can climb out of that," Second Harold stated. "It's been forty years since I had the agility."

"It's not as big as I thought it would be," Laurane complained.

"Jim, you let us out!" Harold yowled. "Dwarf, goblin, pirate, or mermaid, I don't care what you are, you let us out!"

"Seems like the bolt is jammed," Jim replied from the other side. "Best if you lay down and rest for now. I'll be back in a bit!"

"Jim!" Harold shouted, but there was no response.

"Conned!" Second Harold growled.

"We best lay down and rest sweetheart…sweethearts," Laurane spoke softly. "Maybe the Fae are testing us. Testing our faith. If we prove we believe, they will let us go."

Laurane laid on the floor, a concerned look over her face. Harold scowled and joined her. Second and Third Harold copied him. "Look at the mess you got us into!" he complained to her.

"I want more lemonade," Third Harold huffed.

The ground shook as Jim the realtor watched the figure top the distant hills to the West and cross the desert. It took a long time for it to approach, and as the minutes passed by, the figure grew larger and larger. This one was a biggie even by the standards of most fairy folk. Jim was impressed. He'd had to custom tailor the order weeks in advance, but the payment had been worth it. Three entire leprechaun pots!

The figure—Jim's costumer—moved with a strange gait: an unnatural limp from only wearing one shoe over its right foot. The left foot was bare, tire-sized toes covered in dust. As the figure drew close and the ground really began to shake, the elderly voices from inside the house-boot cried in alarm.

"How you doin', Quentin?" Jim called out in Gaelic. Everyone knew giants only spoke Gaelic.

"Doing good. Well as best as can be helped walking around bare-foot," Quentin replied, voice deep and rumbly, like a rockslide in a cave. Jim could barely see Quentin's head way up there in the sky. A gaggle of sprites hung from Quentin's pant legs, chittering and giggling to themselves. Sprites were always bumming free rides from giants. One pointed to Jim and stuck out its tongue. The other sprites roared out in laughter.

"I see you got me a replacement," Quentin boomed out.

"Sure did!" Jim crowed happily. "With the special inserts you needed as well! Extra padding!"

"Extra padding, you say?" Quentin said excitedly. "That's great! The arch on my foot has been killing me! Doctor says I have flat feet."

"You got medical insurance now?" Jim asked. "Fancy for your kind. Must have snagged yourself a good job."

"Lugging these ones around on tours," Quentin answered. He pointed an enormous finger to the sprites.

"Perfect job for you," Jim complimented. "You giants like to hike around."

Quentin shrugged. "Can't ever stay in one place for too long now-a-days."

"Yeah," Jim frowned, "the world sure is changing."

"Sure is," Quentin agreed.

# Caroigne

**Caias Ward**

Blacktooth sniffed the boy. Her bulbous, grey nose pressed against him, the wiry hairs jutting out of it—coarse against the young skin. He was a mix of sickly and delicious, the flavor of a well-fattened and well-muscled farm lad who sweated in his duties and who suffered a creeping illness. She guessed he was sixteen, maybe seventeen. He was easy to overcome, a quick swat to the head, knocking him out but not harming him too much. She towered over him by several feet; he lay on the small table, small to her, at least.

She decided not to cook him, at least for now.

"Wake up," she said, her voice dressed in silk. It had a power behind it, more command than request, ancient magic of the Summer and Winter Courts.

The boy's eyes sprung open. He did not move… he could not, other than the barest rocking of his limbs. He could breathe, and he pushed air out of his mouth before speaking.

"I knew you would not eat me," the boy said.

"How do you know this? How do you know I will not eat you still?"

Blacktooth leaned over the table so the boy could see her. Unwashed, grey ropes of hair framed her twisted shrunken-apple-head and hung down about his face. Her eyes were bright amber with black dots sucking in the light. Her mouth was a greedy cave guarded by a picket of blackened teeth, glossy and sharp. Her lips were thick, cracked and protruding; her gobbly chin and neck were a sparse forest of rigid white hair.

"I'm sick," the boy said, a slight cough interrupting his words. "Got the red pox."

"Don't see no blisters on you," Blacktooth said, roughly pawing the boy, exposing his skin. He was soft on the surface, but she could feel the delicious muscle beneath.

"Don't show no marks," the boy said. "I get a cough, and the sweats in the cold like now, but that's it. Brother said I'mma 'carrier', but I ain't never gonna get really sick from it."

Blacktooth snorted, shuffling away. Her woolen robe was ragged and patched, a disheveled sack on her giant frame. All the boy could see above him was a roof of thatch and wood, sooty smoke reaching for the ceiling, drying parts of things and plants hanging down. It was warm, almost too much, even in the edge of winter. He heard shuffling, clattering, the grinding of mortar and pestle.

He waited, because he could do nothing else.

Blacktooth came back to the table, scooped a dirty paste into the boy's mouth with the ripped claw on her grey thumb. She massaged his throat, forcing him to swallow the bitter mush. He shuddered, his limbs jerking about. She shook him, sat him up, slapped him on his relatively tiny back with her meaty hand. She handed water to him in a massive cup and he drank until his belly swelled. She took the cup and set it on the table, stepping away from him and resting her hands on her hips.

"Your name, boy?"

The boy moved his mouth around, moved his limbs around, brushed his dark hair away from his round face.

"Nerian," he said.

"Your full name, boy," she hissed. He swallowed, nervous.

"Nerian Bauer," the boy said.

"Some call me Blacktooth."

"Yes, I know," Nerian said vacantly. "People speak of the crone who lives in the upland, that she eats the flesh of man," he said with no judgment, "but you can talk with her and if your story is interesting she will use magic of Summer and Winter and Wild to help you. She… I mean, you, have powerful magic, and know many things."

"You aren't very smart, are you?"

"No, ma'am," Nerian said. "I mean, I knew you could help so I went looking for you."

"How did you even find me?" Blacktooth asked as she nattered around her hut. It was cluttered with things made of bone and beast, jars of notions, and dried meats of many kinds. She moved through it easily, picking around for a variety of ingredients.

"I looked for where the animals were afraid. Then for your prints. Hunters swap tales of the hag of the woods…" Blacktooth cocked a shaggy brow at him, and seeing no malice in his choice of words beckoned him to continue. "And I asked where hunters didn't come back. I know the woods, and animals. And then I saw the hut, in the ring of mushrooms."

He nodded as only a simpleton could.

"You saw the hut?" Blacktooth squinted at the boy, sniffing him again.

"Yes. It is not well-hidden."

"You are an innocent," Blacktooth pondered aloud.

"But, begging your pardon," Nerian said, "I came here to—"

"You want a cure for the red pox."

"But how did you know?

Blacktooth tilted her head at Nerian, stunned at his stupidity—no—innocence. No wonder he saw past the glamour, she pondered.

"You told me you had the red pox," Blacktooth hissed. "I reason that your village has it as well."

Nerian nodded.

"You can help?"

"How many in your village, child?"

Nerian thought hard, counting in his head, struggling.

"Fifty families."

"I can cure it," Blacktooth said. "The early frost killed off many of the herbs I need, but I should have enough stowed for that small of a group. But what can you give me?"

"I can give you me," Nerian said.

Blacktooth dragged a bleached-wood chair over from a wall and sat down with a creak. She leaned in, resting the elbows of her overlong arms on her knees, putting her hands to her chin.

"Explain, Nerian."

"Well," Nerian said, "you make the cure for me to bring to my village. I make sure everyone gets well. And then I come back."

Blacktooth laughed, her jowls jangling about as she slapped her meaty thighs.

"Yes, of course! I will make your medicines, you will go back to save your village, and then you will come back here to be eaten by me! Of course, how noble of you!" She threw her arms up, her claws clanking against a dangling drying meat-hunk suspended from a rafter. "You will sacrifice yourself for the good of all!"

Blacktooth spit on the ground.

"Foolish boy," she said.

"I ain't smart," Nerian whispered. "All I got is a strong back and big hands. My brother, he's smart—fixes things, knows the Bible word for word and does these tests to see what plants grow better."

"Tests?" Blacktooth asked.

"He called them that. Little plots of land with different plants. He does things to the soil, sees what grows better. Put pigshit, or lime. Then," Nerian struggled with the ideas, "we put four crops in, and…" he brought his arm around in a loop when he couldn't think of the word, "circle… rotate them each planting. He does things with the animals, too. None of them get sick, and he even helped people too, until the red pox got him. The Bishop's heard about him, come to talk to him about his planting. They want to send him to Leipzig, for schooling.

"I ain't smart," Nerian said again, looking down at his hands. "I just haul dirt and plants around, bring the animals around to graze. All I got is the meat on my bones to give my family. My brother is smart, and if he lives he'll help so many people. If I can give my meat to save him, I will. I'll come back when he's well, or even if it don't work. But I have to hurry. I've already been gone for three days, and it will take time to get back. The pox don't work quick if you are lucky…"

Blacktooth snorted. She believed this simple boy, thought about baking his skin after he came back, rendering his fat into a glaze. She thought about his smart brother, and then how she was going to pop this simple boy's eyeballs in her mouth. She walked over to Nerian, leaning in, nose-to-nose, her hands on either side of the boy's shoulders.

"How old are you?" Blacktooth asked, massaging his broad shoulders, feeling at the meat of them.

"Fourteen," Nerian said.

"You are a very large, stupid, young boy," Blacktooth chided him as she took his hand in her large, clawed grip. "But you will stay until morning. I will make what you need. You will deliver it, and then when your brother is well, or if he passes, you shall return."

"To be eaten," Nerian nodded, knowing his fate.

"You shall return."

Blacktooth nicked the boy's palm with her thumb talon. His palm burned slightly, a drowsiness settling over the boy as the binding of words took hold.

"Words are said, Nerian Bauer, marked with blood," Blacktooth said, "Words will bind, and now you sleep, sweetness."

Blacktooth scooped Nerian into her arms as though he were a succulent baby.

Nerian woke in a makeshift bed—bearskin thrown over lumps of cloth—and to Blacktooth shoving a bowl to his face. It reeked of oils and fats and nettles, burning his nose even from far away.

"Drink this all," she forced it to his lips. He pulled away, but she grabbed him by his head and tilted it back. He was strong, but she twisted his head like a newborn calf, able to reach completely around his head with finger and thumb and hold his mouth open with jagged thick nails. She slowly drained the bowl into his throat, stopping him from moving away as she sang to him.

*Little boy lost, out in the field*
*Sky gone dark, stumble and reel*
*Wind blows hard, light bright ahead*
*Moon and stars, they are your friends*

"You have to drink it all at once, sweetness. It's going to hurt for a bit. Best go have a sit at the outhouse, at the hill path."

She took her hand away. Nerian tried to vomit, but the brew camped angrily in his stomach, stomping about warmly. The warmness spread, and he fought the urge to scratch his sweating skin as he sprung from the bed and raced out of the hut and to the outhouse. He doubled over as he sat, his body rejecting his sickness as he tried not to fall into the large hole under the sitting board. Finally, when nothing more purged, he cleaned up and came outside. Clear of the outhouse, he breathed in the cold air… and did not cough. He breathed in again, and felt his skin, dry in the air. He smiled, watching steam come from his mouth, his breath steady and easy.

"Nerian! Boy!"

Nerian turned to the voice calling down the hill. A small man rode a dark chestnut horse with a strong and wide body. The man was pale, in earthen tones and heavy quilted coat, with an army sword at his side and a snaplock in hand.

"Ernst? Why are you here?"

The horse shuffled back and forth in disquiet, the Bishop's man, Ernst darting his head about. Nerian raced down the hill, then slowed as he saw more men, more horses. They were armed; some with spears, some with swords, all with snaplocks. The horses skittered and shook, feeling this land was not of the world they knew.

"Your brother told us where you went. We must go, boy. This place in the mushroom ring is dangerous," Ernst ducked his head lower as though to hide, "filled with children of Nature and Wild."

"Of course," Nerian said. "I must get the medicine first."

"What?"

"The crone made the medicine for the village. I don't carry the pox anymore."

Nerian smiled, but did not know why Ernst and the others blanched.

"You spoke to it?" Ernst blessed himself.

"Yes," Nerian said. "She made medicine for the whole village."

"The Bishop is sick, and the pox has spread to Monschau. You say it made medicine?"

Nerian nodded.

"We brought extra horses," Ernst said. "If we can find the way out, we can ride back and get more men to take the beast—"

"Beast? No," Nerian said. "She made enough for the village."

"We can help your brother," Ernst said, reaching down to Nerian, "and your family, but the rest must go to the Bishop and those he deems deserve such a blessing." He clasped Nerian's arm. "Now get on the horse with me and we'll ride to the camp."

"No, I promised!" Nerian insisted, yanking away so hard that Ernst tipped in the saddle. He struggled to pull himself upright, his horse snorting as Nerian pushed away and broke into a run. Regaining control, Ernst guided the horse down the hill and up the one next to it, chasing the boy.

Nerian ducked and bobbed through the bare brush, the trees were thicker here. The others followed, picking up the pace, the trees grabbing and pulling at them, slowing the horses.

A snaplock rang out. Ernst cursed at the man who fired; he hoped to calm the boy and avoid the beast. He pressed on, the ground leveling, the ride a bit easier. His mount crashed through thicket and thorn, snorting and heaving. Ernst pulled at his own leg tangled in low branches, watching the boy vanish over a hilltop. The other men passed him, but soon he hacked the branch free with his sword and cleared the rise towards the hut.

Blacktooth bled from her forearm, the shot having passed through; she hunched over from the pain, almost squatting. The man who fired it was a crumpled pile on the frozen ground, his horse shuddering, its legs broken, its entrails falling out. Nerian stood in front of Blacktooth, a stout stick clutched in trembling shivering hands. He brought it back in an exaggerated swing, ready to sweep away the world.

The men struggled to control their horses. Blacktooth looked each horse in the eye, her lips peeled back, her black picket of teeth clashing against each other. Ernst's men tried to level the snaplocks, unable to take aim as their mounts whinnied and jerked against reins, shying away from the crone. Ernst yelled to his men to back away as he calmed his own horse and brought it slowly forward.

"Nerian," Ernst said, "move away from the beast. We can talk about this, all of us."

Nerian stood his ground.

"This is not the first time men have come to kill me as I mind by business," Blacktooth said. "Men often fear what they cannot control. I am no maiden, no woman breeding or bleeding, but I keep my blood and my power within to do magic as I wish, not at a man's command!"

"I know, woman," Ernst said. "Your blood no longer flees you each moon, you fey-touched crone. Nerian said you made powerful medicine."

"They want to take it for the Bishop!" Nerian yelled.

"There is enough for your family," Ernst said.

"But not for the village too," Nerian yelled.

"You need to make choices, boy." Ernst let his arm down, the snaplock to the side. "We can take your goods, and help your family, and help the Bishop and his followers."

"My bargain with the boy was not to help the Bishop," Blacktooth spat, standing taller. "We have made a deal, and he is bound to it by powerful forces he does not even know. Words are said, marked with blood, words will bind, and they have, to his name."

She squeezed her hand on the bleeding arm, the thick black blood creeping out the bullet hole. The blood fell in drops, sizzling in the rime on the ground. Ernst looked away from the crone to the ground, listened to the crack of a frozen stone.

"Blood! The blood!" Ernst yelled.

His men looked around confused, the horses even more agitated.

"Shoot her! The magic is in the blood!"

Blacktooth rose up and swung her arm out, flicking the dripping blood towards Ernst. He hung low on the side of his horse, turning it towards Nerian and Blacktooth. The blood splattered on the horse and Ernst's leg, burning away saddle and clothing, burning away flesh. The horse neighed in agony, its legs collapsing under it. Ernst sprang out of the saddle, crashing to the ground, slamming his hip into the frozen earth. The other riders fired on Blacktooth, powder-smoke choking the air.

She stalked toward two of the riders; her robe streaked with her blood, her shoulder torn, her chest steaming in the cold. She threw her blood out at them, the spray traveling impossibly far and splashing into their horses. Horsehair burned and trees ignited at the touch. The horses fell in shock, the men crushed under them. Blacktooth leaped on them, black claws ripping into horseflesh, and man-flesh, in glee.

"Betray my hospitality? Trespass in my home? Seek to rob my guest to whom I have sworn an oath?" She howled, ragged nails and jet teeth tearing into tender flesh.

Hooves beat down on the ground, a rider with a spear racing at Blacktooth, hoping to catch her from behind. Nerian swung at the horse's legs with his club. The rider pulled his mount into a jump, but Nerian swung upward and connected with the horse's knee. The force of the blow ripped the club from Nerian's grasp, leaving his hands raw. The horse came down from the jump and crumpled under its smashed knee, chest crashing into the ground, the rider flying forward and scraping to a stop. Nerian picked up the broken spear, grasping the three feet of splintered wood topped by a steel head in his bloody hands.

Snaplocks exploded again, two riders with time enough to rush and reload. Blacktooth fell as the lead hit her in the back. Nerian screamed, running over to the riders and jamming the spear into a rider's leg. The man tried to club Nerian with the grip of his snaplock, but Nerian grabbed his arm and dragged him off the horse. Nerian stabbed his foe over and over even as the other rider struck him in his shoulders. Nerian slumped more and more with each blow, but kept his feet for nearly a minute, blindly puncturing the downed rider again and again. Soon, though, his singular focus and his dimwitted rage could not resist the pummeling. He tumbled onto the body, rolling onto his back. The last rider drew his sword, leaning down to swipe at Nerian.

A log larger than Nerian flew through the air, taking the last rider full in the chest, sprawling him off his mount, pulling the horse over with him. The log crushed both man and horse, a hissing wheeze erupting from between the bloody log and the bloody ground. Nerian blinked, dazed. He stood on weak legs, grabbing his dizzy head, looking around at the red-painted terrain. Some horses had run into the wilds, others flailed in shock from their wounds.

Blacktooth stood near an indentation of a fallen tree, the source of the giant log she threw at Ernst's man.

She tumbled onto her backside, then sprawled completely. Nerian swayed back and forth as he moved forward, trying to get to Blacktooth. He stumbled, watching the crone's rich blood spread out onto the ground, mesmerized by the slick patterns it made in the morning cold. Mushrooms sprung from the moistness, her life fleeing her. He shook his head, the throbbing subsiding, using the spear remnant as a cane to shuffle over to Blacktooth.

"Nerian," Ernst called out to him. "We can still help your brother."

Nerian stopped, then pivoted to the voice coming from behind a dead horse. Ernst waved his arm weakly. Nerian stumbled to the blood-burned horse. Coming around it, Nerian saw Ernst's leg crossed over his body awkwardly, pushing at the horseflesh. His other leg was trapped under the horse, the weight pinning Ernst.

"Boy, help me from under here. We can get the medicine to your brother."

Nerian shuffled closer, and stopped. Ernst pushed more, then stopped as he waited for the boy.

"My brother, and the village?"

"Your family, yes," Ernst evaded.

Nerian came close.

"The village?"

"Nerian, the Bishop is sick. And he has so much work left to do in this world—"

Nerian shoved the spear into Ernst's chest. His mouth went small, his voice gurgled. Soon, Ernst was quiet, and Nerian worked his way over to Blacktooth.

Blacktooth coughed in the warm hut, bundled in blankets, wracked in pain. Nerian squeezed a sponge into her mouth, the liquid warm and tasty. She was propped up, halfway sitting up.

"You caught a fever, but it went quick," Nerian said. "You remember eating?"

Blacktooth thought through the pain, remembering… chewing? Using the chamber pot to the side of the bed?

"I got you into the hut, sewed up the wounds, took a guess on what would help you," Nerian said. "Then used some of the herbs I recognized, ones my brother used on the animals. Found a horse and tried out your poultices. One healed up a wound nice and quick. Sometimes things stick in my head. Glad I remember some."

Nerian swapped from the sponge to a spoon. He scooped up stew from another bowl, holding it up to Blacktooth, putting it into her mouth.

"How many days passed?"

"Been a week," Nerian said. "I was away, bringing the medicine to the village, but I rode hard and quick. I made sure you had enough to eat in case I couldn't get back."

"Your brother—"

"He's fine now. The village too. We lost a few, but most are good."

Blacktooth nodded.

"But it was just like cutting up the hogs," Nerian said and offered another spoonful to her.

"What was?" Blacktooth asked. She sucked the soup down.

"Ernst, and the men. I knew you would be hungry. Needed to keep your strength. You lost blood, and used lots of it, to protect us. So I butchered them, cooked them up for you. Figured it would help, with the mushrooms from your blood."

Blacktooth tilted her head, thinking.

"You sweet boy... you nursed me back to health."

"I told you I ain't got nothing but my meat," Nerian said. "And even though I didn't feel the pull of the words and the blood, since you were so sickly, I promised. And that's *my* word. So I came back."

Nerian climbed down from the bed, went to the fire, pulling a roast away, cutting and carving, bringing the plate to Blacktooth. He handed the plate up to Blacktooth. She struggled to take it, but breathed it in. Gingerly, she reached to the plate, stabbing meat with her claws, shoveling it into her mouth.

"I'm thinking there's enough meat between the horses and the men," Nerian dared to mention.

Blacktooth laughed, looking at the boy as she speared more meat and tossed it into her maw.

"You can go, boy. I never bound you to let me eat you. Just to come back."

"Why did you want me to come back?"

"It's lonely here. And even old women like me miss people."

"I can visit, if you like? Maybe help you until you get better? And maybe you can teach me. I'm not smart, but sometimes things stick."

Blacktooth chuckled, dragging her gobbet-coated claws across her tongue, savoring the meat and juices.

"I would like that, sweetness."

END of Grifty Shades of Fey: Volume One
Discover more great fiction at
www.fvpress.com

## Greetings from Fiction Vortex

IF YOU HAVE GOTTEN this far, hopefully you are looking forward to reading more of A Grifty Shades of Fey Anthology and other Fiction Vortex™ StoryVerses™. You're in luck! We have an official butt-load of episodes available. Head on over to www.fvpress.com to get all the latest.

Fiction Vortex is all about episodic fiction like the stuff you just read. We are powered by the collaborative writing software known as StoryShop (a project we have helped birth in order to spread our fiction faster!) Thus far, our StoryVerses™ have been a crazy stupid success, but our baby is still so young and frail!

It's time to suckle the milk of brilliant genre fiction until our bones grow strong enough to withstand the slings and arrows of traditional publishing's lumbering giant. At Fiction Vortex™, we are so brazen to assume we can, nay WILL, pioneer the future of digital storytelling. We scoff at the idea of ebooks being the end all of digital publishing.

Let's work together to restore the intimate bonds and direct collaboration between storyteller and audience. Let's use the technology at our fingertips to do so. Become an integral part in discovering the new balance in written storytelling—a balance forged by reader and writer together.

Made in the USA
San Bernardino, CA
16 February 2020

64484077R00153